Grava

The huge, purple planet hung menacing and low on the horizon as Commander Darek Jarrod stepped from the vehicle that had brought him from his home on the other side of the Capital.

As his transport bulleted silently away, he crossed the square purposefully, his heels resounding from the smooth metal walls of the high, domed buildings that surrounded him on three sides. He made his way to the central and more dominant one, and climbed the slope to its entrance, the surface beneath his feet buckling neatly into an instant step with each stride he made, only to flatten, silently, level once again in his wake.

The one-piece tunic he wore shimmered in the glow of the vast planet hanging, seemingly, so close that it could be touched, as his slim, muscular legs powered him effortlessly to the top. Once there, with the entrance to the Congress Building before him, he hesitated, brushed the long blond hair back from his high forehead, and turned to look over the sprawling megalopolis. The hush that hung there only added to its beauty, the clean, wide boulevards neatly bisecting the parklands, the cloverleaf switchbacks which would normally be thronged with people going about their business standing virtually deserted, like discarded ribbons from a child's hair.

This Citadel, Jarrod knew, was now typical of all habitation-clusters on his planet, depleted and depeopled, with those as yet unaffected by the disease afraid to venture out from their sterilized homes for fear of infection. Grava was fast becoming a depopulated planet as the Sporon spread insidiously.

The silence was ominous, broken only by the periodic crackle and flare of laser rounds filtering down from the sky as they broke against the outer exclusion shield protecting them from the sniper fire from Omnia. Jarrod turned hate-filled eyes towards the purple orb, and despaired yet again at the wickedness of such a race as the Omnians, who, not content with keeping up their futile, one-sided war with Grava for countless generations, had now, it would seem, committed the ultimate act of evil in planting the killer disease upon his planet.

There was, of course, no evidence that it was the

work of Omnia; there could never be a denial from them because, despite repeated attempts at reconciliation by Grava, the Omnians had never, ever, communicated. But Jarrod knew, as did the rest of the Governing Council with whom he was about to meet, that the return of the dreaded Sporon was no accident. That's what made it all such a bitter pill to swallow, the fact that it was a disease for which the Gravatites had once, in their distant past, had a cure. But that had been far back in the Days of Legend, when things like sickness, crime and pollution had been a part of their world.

The Old Books said that it had been whilst the scientists had been researching a cure for the Sporon that they had created the alternative substance, Kracka, which, within ten moonruns, had eradicated all known diseases and illnesses.

The story was as old as the heavens themselves, and to be truthful, it was so much a part of Grava mythology that not everyone believed it, but what *was* undeniable was that, today, the only killers of Gravatites were old age, accident, and the occasional incursion by the odd, fanatical Omnian. Until now, that is, until one moonphase ago when the first deaths from Sporon began to be registered, and now there was not one scientist on the planet who wouldn't give everything for just one drop of that original, forgotten cure.

* * *

Jarrod turned and strode resolutely into the building, making for the ascender which would take him to level 200, where an area the size of a small town had been set aside by the governor to deal with all aspects of the Sporon emergency.

He was not sure why they had sent for him; his own speciality was galaxy exploration, and he couldn't quite see, as yet, how that might fit in with a resolution to the crisis.

There was a man waiting for him by the exit to level 200 who had been sent to escort him to the operations bay, and together they followed a corridor past the vastness of the Medical Research Unit. The Unit had been hastily put together and staffed by those scientists thought most likely to be able to grapple with some success with the long-forgotten intricacies of medicine. Even the sign saying "Medical Research" was strange to see. It was the one area of science for which there had been no call for a whole millenium, and considering that no records existed from the time of the original Sporon outbreak, these scientists were, literally, relying on guesswork to find a cure.

The rest of the Governing Council were assembled when Jarrod was brought in.

At the table sat the governor, concern written clearly on his face, and with him were nine others, all commanders like Jarrod, though not in the military sense. Despite the continued aggression by Omnia, Grava had no military strategy.

It was not a policy that Jarrod particularly agreed with, but he grudgingly acknowledged that, if a policy of non-aggression was to succeed, then it had to exclude *all* forms of aggression, and if that meant not fighting back against Omnia, then, however unwillingly, he knew he had to accept it.

Jarrod was puzzled to see a hologram in the shape of an exploratory Starship hovering over the centre of the table; it was turning constantly, so that everyone could see it from all sides. It was not one of recent design; its style dated back many hundreds of moonruns. It was circular, as the early ships used to be, as opposed to the flat, elongated, round-ended ships currently being used for space exploration; and it was domed, which dated it back almost to the Days of Legend, but what really pinpointed the era which it came from was its colour. Its bright, iridescent green characterized the metal from which it was made, a metal which, Jarrod knew, had ceased to be used in such ships at least twenty generations ago.

Jarrod was not a regular member of the Governing Council. His status earned him the right to a seat at the table, but his work often took him to the far corners of the universe and beyond, where he was able to study and report on the various life forms he found. Consequently, the only face he really recognized at the table, apart from the governor himself, was his friend Drago.

He and Drago had been at the Academy of Ballistics together before fate had moved them in different directions, Jarrod into exploration, Drago into politics, but their friendship went back much further than that, to a place on the far side of the planet where they had both grown up. In that carefree time, they had shared everything, especially a love for their world. This had eventually brought the two of them here to Grava's great Capital, to study, in order to try to find a way in which they could contribute to Grava's welfare, and the welfare of its people.

Jarrod took the empty chair, nodded acknowledgement of the welcome from the governor, and listened politely as Drago introduced the rest of the assembled group. There was an eagerness about the others which baffled Jarrod; it was almost as though his presence was a signal for optimism. He caught Drago's eye and frowned his curiosity, but his friend merely shrugged "wait and see".

"Commander Jarrod," began the governor, when they had all settled. "You are familiar with the type of Starship which you see projected here?"

Jarrod nodded. "Class six, early 'B' model; DX sequence; Kropkametal construction; minimum lightspeed capabilities; crew of twenty-four; in service from approximately generation thirty, became obsolete from around generation thirty-six. The Spaceflight Museum has one just like it."

The governor caused the hologram to rotate to a point where its identity number became clear. "Does this particular type of ship mean anything to you?" he asked.

Jarrod read the number: DX900. What was familiar about that number sequence? He searched his memory. "Were not the DX vessels the first ones to discover the Nine Planet System?" he asked.

"They were indeed," agreed the governor, "and the first to bring back detailed information of the one planet in that system capable of sustaining life similar to ours."

"The planet Earth," smiled Jarrod. "I know it well, visit it regularly as part of our information update programme."

"That," said the governor, "is one of the reasons you are here, Commander."

Jarrod was beginning to wish he would come to the point.

"Tell me," the governor went on, "is there anything about this particular ship which stirs a memory?"

Jarrod frowned. The DX900 ... 900 ... there *was* something he ought to remember ... but what was it? Of course! The only ship to have crashed on the surface of a foreign planet! There had been many lost in space over the generations, victims of meteor storms, or pressure failure and such, but the DX900 was unique in Grava history for that reason.

"The DX900," said Jarrod, "failed to return from Earth in, I think, generation thirty fifty-two."

"Fifty-three," corrected the governor.

His pernicketiness irritated Jarrod. "Forgive me, governor," he said, "but as yet I fail to see how this can have a bearing on the current Omnian problem – assuming that it is the Omnian problem I have been brought here to discuss?"

Drago recognized the annoyance in Jarrod's tone; he had heard it often in discussion whenever Omnia was mentioned.

He and Jarrod thought alike when it came to Omnia. Their dearest wish had always been to find a solution to the dispute that had been raging with Omnia for as long as time itself. A peaceful solution would, of course, be preferable, but both Drago and Jarrod had always agreed between themselves that the governmental policy of non-aggression could not be the only choice they had. Given the chance they would hit back at the Omnians, and it was frustrating to think that they would probably never get that chance. Jarrod's frustration was beginning to show now, and Drago stepped in.

"If the governor will allow me...?"

The governor nodded his agreement, and Drago turned to his friend.

"Commander Jarrod, at the time of the first plague

of Sporon, all those generations ago, the DX type Starships carried a supply of the cure Kracka, for the safety of the crew. DX900 also had its supply, carried in a phial by the ship's medical officer."

He rose from the table and strode casually along behind the seated men.

"When the DX900 crashed on Earth in generation thirty fifty-three – the year 894 AD as it was on Earth – that phial, and the cure, survived."

"We know this for certain," put in the governor. "Shortly before the DX900 disintegrated, its captain emptied the ship's memory banks into our computers here on Grava; we have that transmission on record."

Drago once again took up the tale. "As you know, automatically, along with a transmission of that kind, comes a status report on the ship, and you know how detailed *that* can be..."

Indeed Jarrod did. Such a report would even detail the number of writing and eating utensils that should be on board, and any less than that number would immediately show.

"The status report from the DX900 showed that the phial containing the cure was missing. More than that, it showed that the DX900's onboard computers had already located the phial on the surface of the planet. We believe that the ship was manoeuvring to return to the surface to retrieve the phial when it blew up."

There was a pause. The governor dismissed the

hologram, and Drago returned to his seat. They were obviously waiting for a reaction from Jarrod, and to be honest, Jarrod was not at all sure what sort of reaction was expected.

"If I hear you correctly," he began, "you are telling me that a sample of the cure for the Sporon disease exists – on Earth?"

"Exactly."

Jarrod continued, "But that it exists in Earth's history . . . in the year. . ."

"894 AD," said Drago.

Jarrod gave a hollow laugh. "Then what use is it to us?"

"None," said the governor, "unless it can be retrieved."

"Over one thousand Earth years later? Impossible! I know the Earth, I know what the Earth does to metals buried in it. Even if we located it, corrosion would have eaten the phial away long, long ago, particularly a metal such as Kropka. All that would be left would be green, flaky dust."

Drago leaned forward; fixed his friend with a knowing smile. "But if we were to retrieve the phial at the moment of its loss. . ."

For a moment, Jarrod thought that Drago was being flippant, but a glance at the other faces in the room told him differently. "You mean . . . go back in time?"

Drago nodded, the smile still playing about his lips.

"But we can't do that," retorted Jarrod, "it's been tried, many times..."

A voice from a dark corner of the room made Jarrod jerk his head sharply in that direction: "*We* can't do it, but Earthlings can."

Jarrod recognized the speaker as he stepped from the shadows, and his face hardened. He was a young man, almost as tall as himself, with aristocratic features, a cruel nose and humourless eyes. He was a man who had made many of the same journeys to Earth as Jarrod, a physiologist of great promise, and also of great ambition.

"Silak Tulkan."

Tulkan smiled and inclined his head. Their dislike for each other was well known, and had he been at the table Jarrod might well have reacted badly.

On more than one occasion he and Jarrod had disagreed violently on points of ethics. Tulkan had a reputation for getting things done whatever the cost.

The governor spoke. "Tulkan knows the physiology of the Earth humans better than anyone; perhaps he should explain."

Tulkan shrugged, and his smile widened. "Quite simply," he said, "although our own bodies, with their ferrous composition, disintegrate when ejected into reverse, the Earthlings, with their chromosomatic metabolism, have no such problem. Because they have a *biological* link to the past, as opposed to our mineral links, there is an inbuilt degree of flexibility which promotes cellular adaption to changes – they *can* travel through time."

Jarrod waited, but Tulkan had obviously said his piece. He swung his chair to face the young scientist. "I think you may be overlooking one thing," he said evenly. "Earthlings are like us only in physical appearance. I have studied them for two whole generations. They have a will and a reasoning and a self-imposed freedom of choice which affects every decision they make. They have no need to do as we wish. What reason would any Earthling have to help us?"

Drago interjected. "There is, in fact, just *one* person who can help us retrieve the phial."

"One?"

Drago nodded. "The direct descendant of the person who, in 894 AD, found the phial."

"It is as I said," interrupted Tulkan. "Because there is a chromosomatic link, the genetic make up of the holder of the phial can be aligned with that of his descendant, acting as a continuum, and thus enabling a time transference to take place. The link, if you will, forms a 'tunnel' down which he can be projected."

"And as *I* said, Tulkan," returned Jarrod, "this person, whoever he is, has no need to involve himself."

"He simply needs to be persuaded," said Tulkan.

"Everyone here seems to think that you can persuade him."

He didn't add "I don't", but that was what his tone implied.

Shaun

It had been a heavy day, but interesting.

Shaun sat back on his heels and wiped an arm across his brow, a glow of satisfaction building as he ran his eyes over the thirty or so shards of broken pot that he had painstakingly unearthed since he began that morning. He put aside his brush and trowel and picked up the largest piece again, examining it for the umpteenth time.

It had been a part of the shoulder of the pot, and still had a loop handle attached. A flick from his nail produced a sound which confirmed his first assessment, that the clay had been fired to a low temperature, probably around 800 degrees centigrade. It was unglazed, but had been burnished, and most wonderful of all, along where the handle had been smoothed in as wet clay, were distinct fingerprints, the prints of the Saxon maker of the pot, fired into the clay over a thousand years ago, and still as clear as the day they were made.

Shaun fitted his own fingers over the prints, imagining what it must have been like to have been the man, or woman, who had fashioned the vessel; he looked at the shape of his own hand, and knew that the maker must have held his hand in just the same way.

For most of the day, Shaun had been searching for the matching shoulder of the pot, always assuming it was still in one piece, but so far it had eluded him, and now it was getting a bit late in the day to continue much longer. Maybe tomorrow would bring more luck.

There were times when Shaun couldn't actually believe the luck he'd already had, like when this archaeological dig, over the site of a Saxon village, had opened up, only half a mile from his home. His interest in archaeology had stemmed from his interest in history, particularly early English history. The coastal land around where he lived, the town of Rufford, was especially rich in it. The East Anglian coast was the one that had been most heavily plundered by the Danes and Vikings in the years leading up to 1000 AD, and for a seventeen-year-old budding archaeologist it was a treasureland of information and discovery.

His own family had lived in these parts for centuries; he knew that from the genealogical enquiries he'd made, mostly from the record books kept at the Town Hall. They knew him well down at the Town Hall, where the clerks and secretaries good-humouredly called him "Bloodnut", because of his copper-red hair. He didn't mind, most people with red hair were ribbed from time to time about it; besides, he was proud of his hair, it had been a feature of the family for generations.

The late afternoon sun cast a momentary shadow over him, and looking to his right, he saw that a man had knelt to work not one metre away. He was slim with long, blond hair swept back from a high forehead, and in his early forties, Shaun reckoned. His overalls were remarkably clean considering they were coming to the end of a day's dig. He was a stranger to Shaun, though with new people joining the group daily, he couldn't know them all. Mostly they were keen amateurs, anxious to be of assistance, and they usually got terribly over-enthusiastic at the first sign of anything even remotely old.

Somehow, this man didn't look like an amateur. He turned his head and smiled at Shaun, before pursing his lips and nodding appreciation of the pile of shards stacked between them. The way he held himself as he worked suggested to Shaun a dedication that he hadn't noticed amongst any of the other workers, and Shaun got a strong feeling that he was in the presence of somebody whose passion for the past might well match his own.

They worked for a while in silence, scraping and brushing, but Shaun found he couldn't concentrate on what he was doing. He found his eyes were wandering over to the new arrival, who was working intently, as if nothing was as important as the patch of earth he was scraping at. In the end, Shaun abandoned his own efforts, and watched the man. He was working the ground like a surgeon doing an operation. Shaun saw that, gradually, he was uncovering something; being exposed bit by bit was what looked remarkably like the matching shoulder and loop handle of the pot which he himself had been excavating. It was almost as though the man had known exactly where to dig!

But that was impossible! Whatever was found was only happenstance.

Shaun stumped across on his knees.

"May I?" he said, and as the man nodded, smiling, Shaun set to eagerly, helping to retrieve the missing piece; he and the stranger working at it, carefully, from opposite ends.

"This will probably complete the pot," breathed Shaun. "I think I've got most of the remainder there."

"So I see," said the man. "You seem to have a talent for this."

"I don't know about that," said Shaun. "Just a

fascination." He held his breath as the piece moved, slightly loose. "I hope to study it at University if I do well enough in my 'A' levels."

Their faces were centimetres apart now, their efforts combined in the one task.

"And how long have you had this 'fascination'?"

"For as long as I can remember."

"Many people think that what is past should be forgotten," said the stranger.

"Not me," replied Shaun. "I don't think mankind can plan ahead without knowing what's gone on before, do you?"

"In other words," said the man, ignoring the question, "what has happened in the past can affect the future?"

Shaun shook his head. "Not 'can'– 'will'. Bound to if you think about it."

"Interesting."

The piece lifted without cracking, and Shaun gently carried it over to the matching piece in the pile, a smile lighting his face. The two shoulders fitted together so perfectly it was almost unbelievable; never had he seen a joint so undetectable; no chips along the edge, nothing to suggest, as on the other pieces, that the pot had shattered. It could almost have been machine-made to fit.

The new piece also had a raised stamp, a piece into which the maker had pressed his emblem when it had been wet clay. Shaun peered closer, brushing away the dirt. This was a real find; pots with identification marks were rare for this period.

It was a symbol, and at first he couldn't make out what it was; then he realized it had been impressed upside down. Quickly, he turned it around, and his heart leapt at what he saw.

It was crudely carved, but nevertheless recognizable; Shaun had seen the same symbol endless times on his visits to the Town Hall: an owl above two swords inside a shield – the coat of arms of his town, Rufford!

But there was something else which caused him to blink and stare closer, a word, just discernible, in Old English: "OSWOLDBEARN" – Son of Oswold.

Shaun's jaw dropped.

Oswoldson was Shaun's surname.

"Look at this!" he cried, and turned to show the find to the stranger.

But the stranger had gone.

It was an hour later, just as the sun was beginning to settle on the horizon, that Shaun left the site and made his way home. His find had been admired by everyone, and the coincidence of finding his own name on the pot, all agreed, had been an astounding stroke of luck. A chance in a million.

Shaun had listened to the enthusiastic comments from the rest of the team, and had nodded and agreed, but with something of a sense of detachment.

It could almost have been someone else they were talking about. He felt a sense of unreality about the whole incident: from the arrival of the stranger, through their short conversation, to the finding of the (too perfect) shoulder of the pot – with *his* name upon it . . . it was all just *too* coincidental somehow, too . . . too . . . there wasn't a word for the feeling he felt.

Where had the man come from? And where had he gone to so quickly?

He hadn't been around at the end of the day when the diggers had gathered to secure the site.

Who was he?

Shaun turned the corner, passed under the viaduct, and into Hardiman Street.

Roadworks! Not even room for pedestrians.

He continued, with the intention of turning left at the end of the road he was now on, Portland Avenue, then left again, which would bring him out at the far end of his own street.

His footsteps echoed flatly from the wall as he hurried along, pleased, despite his reservations, with the find he'd made. He'd often thought of himself as a person "out of time", someone who *should* have lived then, in those times that had so much attraction for him. Perhaps he had done. If what they say about reincarnation is true, perhaps the Oswoldson who had owned the pot had been himself in a former life.

He laughed to himself at the thought.

He came to the end of Portland Avenue, and turned left.

More roadworks!

"What's going on?" he muttered. "Surely they could leave enough room to walk by!"

Apparently not.

He continued, and found that a short way further along, the road narrowed into a back-street on to which, to his right, the rear doors of a block of houses opened. The street was cobbled, and so narrow that, had he wished to do so, he could have reached out and touched both sides at the same time.

He stopped and reviewed his situation. He wasn't quite sure which street he was at the back of, but if he kept on along here, he should be able to cut around the block and find himself on Great Rumney Road, the main thoroughfare.

His love affair with the English language had been going on almost from the day that he discovered, as an infant, that words had meaning, but unlike those who liked to use words to convey emotions or feelings, Shaun's interest had always lain in the mechanics of language, its roots, its origins, its development. It never ceased to amaze him that a language which grew up in such a tiny country as England had spread to become the current major commercial language of the world. There was no doubting that the English race had done much over the last five hundred years, through its exploring and conquering, to shape the way things were today – much like the Greeks had done, and the Romans, in their time.

He often wondered what his world, today's world, would have been like if the English language hadn't survived, as indeed, it very nearly hadn't. At one time, the Old English language, the basis of the English spoken today, had been spoken only in one small corner of the country, when the British Isles had been under the almost total rule of the Danish, Swedish and Norwegian Vikings.

He trudged on, beginning to feel the cold now, and a watery fog was starting to build up as the light faded. Then, the wall on his left ended quite suddenly, and he found himself walking by the side of a field. The mist that was spreading from it swirled eerily with the movement of his legs.

A field?

He didn't know there was a field in this area. He could have sworn he knew every piece of spare land in the neighbourhood.

The mist began to thicken. Sudden fogs such as this were fairly common in this part of the country, at this time of the year. He'd seen them happen before on the open fens.

Suddenly, very suddenly, the row of identical doors on his right ended, and he found himself looking into . . . nothing!

The fog, billowing now, made it difficult to judge

distance, so that his eyes could have been focusing long or short – it was impossible to say. As it happened, it didn't matter because he couldn't make out any shapes at all.

He groped backwards for the end of the building he had just passed – and grasped empty air!

Treading cautiously, one step at a time, reaching, he felt sure he must be by the building now – still nothing.

He was now completely disorientated; it no longer mattered in which direction he moved, as slowly, arms outstretched, he shuffled forwards through the clammy murk, cursing his luck under his breath.

The sound of his footsteps, flat and unresonant, told him that he was out in the open. There was nothing, neither sight nor sound, to suggest that there were buildings or objects of any kind at hand.

He may as well have been walking blindfold on the moon. He felt annoyance rather than alarm, knowing that his house could only be a matter of metres from him.

Twenty or thirty paces further on, he stopped, listening, his breath making quick clouds before his face, straining his eyes. Had he imagined it, or had he heard the sound?

A sort of tinkle, like the sound of metal on stone.

The silence felt like a weight. How long he stood there he couldn't tell, until – Yes! there it was again! Dead ahead! He listened once more; heard it once more, and slowly realized that, almost without knowing it, he was inching forward towards the sound. In the absence of any other stimulation, it was the only option he had.

"Hello?" he shouted.

No response.

Then, faintly, he saw it – a glimmer of light.

Ten more paces revealed that it was coming from a high window some metres in front of him. He edged forward more rapidly, relief flooding over him.

It was about eight metres from the lighted window that Shaun stumbled over the first of a flight of stone steps leading up to it. He began to mount them falteringly. A brief break in the fog showed him stone pillars, strangely familiar he thought, on either side of the steps, and from one of them, swinging lightly, hung a chain. He tapped it, and the familiar tinkle he had been following rang out clearly.

But why was the chain moving at all? There wasn't a breath of wind, and yet its sound had led him to this spot. As he reached the topmost step, he saw that the window from which the light was shining was above a huge, carved wooden door, and chiselled upon the stone plinth above the door, were words in gold letters.

Unbelievable words!

A name. The name of the building on whose steps he was now standing.

He drew breath sharply as he read:

"RUFFORD TOWN HALL."

Sheer disbelief made his head buzz, and he leaned against the wall for support, giving his senses a chance to clear and to accept what he knew to be an impossibility.

He leaned back and read again the words above his head. There was no mistake.

This, however impossible, was Rufford Town Hall; the same Town Hall which he knew to be on the other side of the Great Rumney Road, on the far side of the town, and in totally the opposite direction from that in which he had been forced to walk by the inconvenient road works.

Where had he gone wrong? How had what little sense of direction he had let him down so ... so completely?

He took his mind back over his journey from the excavation site, picturing each turning he had taken and imagining the route he would have walked had he not been diverted – twice. Then he had come to the field. The field – that was what had really thrown him.

The more he thought about it, the more certain he felt that the field should not have been there! But, then again, neither should the Town Hall, yet here he was, standing outside its very door.

There was no way he could have lost his way to that degree. He came back to cold, damp reality and surveyed his situation. He had to make a move, he knew that much. Looking behind him all he could see was the swirling, yellow fog, thicker now if anything, and very, very uninviting. If he could be sure of what he would be able to find out there, buildings or roads that he knew, he would attempt to grope his way through it, but that would still leave him with the problem of how he had come to be where he was. It did seem almost as though he had been led here, as though "fate", whatever that was, had brought him here.

If so – why? Was it a dream? Had the whole day been a dream?

"Town Hall," he murmured to himself, "Town Hall . . . why the Town Hall?"

He had to know. He cast another glance down the foggy stone steps, then turned to the door before him.

He was going in. With his heartbeat throbbing in his temples, he pushed the door open and stepped inside.

Everything was surprisingly normal. He felt the stuffy warmth of the building envelop him, and caught the familiar smell of books, polish and old paper. Pushing his way cautiously through the glass-panelled swing doors he found himself in the short, broad corridor which opened out, a little further along, into the reception area.

There were offices on either side of the corridor, and as he inched along, he could see, through the glass of the doors, the typists and secretaries busy at work. Office sounds – chattering typewriters, the rustle of paper, the clatter of filing cabinets – percolated through the building; nothing could have been in sharper contrast to the grim scene he had just left outside, and the first pangs of doubt began to gnaw at him.

Was he being a fool?

Was it possible that, in the fog, he had simply walked further than he thought?

He could see that the reception area had a counter of polished wood which ran its whole length, and which was divided by signs hanging above it into sections: "Accounts", "Council Tax", "Licences".

There was no one at the counter, and no one behind it.

The stairs which ran off to the left, he knew, led to the reference section.

He tried the handle on the nearest door; perhaps one of the office workers he could see in there could enlighten him. He felt that the sound of a human voice would certainly help right now.

The handle just turned round and round in his hand.

He pushed against the door, but there was no movement at all, though the rattle it gave should have alerted the people inside.

No one seemed to notice.

Shaun rattled the door again, knocked on the window, quietly at first, then harder.

To his amazement, not one of the people inside, just a metre or so away from him, even turned their heads in his direction.

What *was* happening to him? This was unreal!

It was as though he didn't exist.

And then he noticed the window above the front door.

It was the same, arched window through which he had seen the light in the fog, and what he saw through it now caused him to catch his breath sharply.

There was a blue sky, white clouds, and in the distance, birds flying. To all appearances, outside it was a beautiful day. Where was the fog? Even discounting the fog, at this time of the day it would be twilight.

The sight struck him like a blow in the chest. He ran to the door, his boots clattering over the marble floor, and flung it open.

Fog!

So thick now that he couldn't see the top of the steps he had just climbed up.

He closed the door quickly, leaned his forehead against it, fighting to control the panic which rose in his throat, and took three or four deep, calming breaths. It was some moments before he felt able to move, and when he did it was to whirl in response to a voice quite close behind.

"Can I help you?"

There was an emphasis on the "I". Shaun found himself looking at a tall, angular man in a pin-striped suit. He had long, finely chiselled features, and black hair, shiny and swept straight back from his forehead. His most noticeable feature was his eyes, small and close-set, and the most brilliant blue, almost a turquoise, that Shaun had ever seen.

"Yes," said Shaun, hesitantly, "Yes ... perhaps. You see, I ... er..." He gave a short laugh of embarrassment. "I seem to be lost."

There was something about the man, his manner, his sober dress perhaps, that prevented Shaun from feeling that he was a threat. Coolly, almost casually, the man turned, walked a couple of paces, then looked back over his shoulder, saying, "Please come with me."

He turned on his heel and strode off quickly down the corridor. Shaun hesitated, then, as the man turned behind the counter, he followed.

Somehow – he didn't know why – he felt he had to.

Town Hall

Shaun followed the man through a doorway set in the back wall. His companion strode swiftly, swinging his arms, not looking back once, and Shaun found he had to come up with his own best stride in order to keep within a metre of him.

The corridor they had entered was long, narrow and quite bare. After they had been walking for a minute or so, it gave way to a more primitive passage, the smooth plaster walls becoming sandstone rock. It began to bend and turn, so that, on the odd occasion that Shaun was able to see beyond the man, he could see no distance at all, merely as far as the next curve. It was quite brightly lit, but there appeared to be no light fittings, and the overall "glow" threw no shadows.

They strode on in a silence broken only by the sound of their footsteps, and soon Shaun became aware of a low hum, as though from machinery, which grew louder as they progressed. The passageway ahead straightened a little, and beyond, through the man's swinging arms, Shaun thought he could make out a brighter glow. Strange as the situation was, his instincts still told him that he was not in any danger. He was driven by a desire to know what the outcome of all this would be.

Quite suddenly they reached the end of the passage. A blank wall faced them, and Shaun's companion turned sharply right, took two more paces, and stopped.

Shaun stepped up alongside him, and found himself looking upon the most unlikely and fantastic scene.

They were overlooking an enormous cavern, brightly lit, around which ran a railed ledge on a level with the platform they were standing on. The ledge led, from either left or right of them, to what looked like a room set in the wall on the far side of the cavern. The room had a large window, through which Shaun could see figures moving.

About fifty metres below, the cavern floor was a mass of machinery and controls, attended by men in dull-silver zip-suits. Bright pinpoints of light on the assembled machines flashed and faded in accompaniment to the steady hum that Shaun had heard on his approach.

It was like a scene from a sci-fi movie, except that this was no film.

Central to the activity below was a pod-like object, an elongated egg shape which Shaun guessed was some two to three metres long. It was smooth and featureless, with an incandescent surface remarkably like the mother-of-pearl handle of the penknife he had been given for a birthday as a child. The whole scene filled Shaun with some awe, and not a little trepidation, and for the first time since he had been in the fog, he began to feel slight apprehension.

Where did he, Shaun Oswoldson, fit into a scenario like this? Why was someone going to such great lengths to involve him in a business which was beginning to take on the proportions of a major mystery?

He became suddenly aware of movement behind him, and turned in time to see the man he had followed disappear back down the passage.

The moment he vanished, his place was taken by a figure which literally stepped from the shadow of a rock and stood facing him.

The newcomer was a tall woman, with silver-blonde hair swept back into a pleat, wearing a zip-suit which had a bright red stripe around the top of her right arm.

She took Shaun's arm in one hand, and with the

other, indicated the ledge which encircled the cavern.

There was no mistaking the unspoken request.

Shaun was relieved to find that the ledge was wider than he had thought, but even so, he felt it necessary to hold the rail as he walked ahead of his new guide. Their destination was obvious.

The ledge led only to the far room he had observed, and it was only a matter of a minute before they reached it.

A door slid open as they approached, and stepping through, Shaun found himself in a room which appeared to have been constructed entirely from a smooth, dull-silvery metal. Ceiling, walls, floor, fittings, all had the same satin-like metallic surface, whilst around the walls lay computerized machines, flickering and blurping their information to a man who sat in a central chair, his back to the door. The blonde woman turned, and slid quietly from the room.

Shaun looked closely at the man in the chair, whose zip-suit was a dull gold and carried three red stripes around the arm, and who, so far, had given no indication that he knew that Shaun was even present.

There was something familiar about his build. Shaun watched as the chair containing the gold-suited man slowly turned towards him.

If the chair had contained the Queen of England, Shaun could not have been more surprised. As it was, he could only blink in disbelief as he found himself looking into the face of the stranger who had knelt beside him at the dig.

"Hello, Shaun," he said. "We've been expecting you."

Shaun stared, then turned and stepped up to where the door had been, and searched for a gap, any indication of a way out. Suddenly, he didn't want any of this any more.

The wall was blank.

"I don't know what your idea is, mister," he breathed, "but I don't think I want to. How do I get out of here?"

"You're here now," replied the man, "you might as well know the rest of it..."

Shaun eyed him, defence his main concern now.

"...don't you think?"

He pointed to a chair, but Shaun stood his ground. There was a movement to his left, and a small, square section of the floor rose in a column to his waist height, and on it was a beaker full of liquid.

"This will refresh you," the man explained with a nod. "Drink it."

"Drink it yourself," Shaun muttered warily.

The man leaned back in his chair and gave Shaun an encouraging smile. "Shaun..." he began.

"How do you know my name?" Shaun interrupted.

"First things first," the man replied. "You can call me Jarrod."

"I could think of a couple of things I could call you, mister," said Shaun, defensively. "You knew I was coming all the time, didn't you?"

"We arranged it."

"Arranged?"

"The fog ... the roadworks – hallucinations."

It took a moment for Shaun to take in what Jarrod was saying, and, by then, Jarrod was speaking again. "We had to be sure we had your exclusive attention. We had to bring you here, to see, so that you could know that what we have to tell you is not fantasy."

"You lead me to a building that I knew shouldn't be there, and you don't call that fantasy?"

"It was a building you were familiar with," explained Jarrod, "and at that time, you were in need of reassurance; also, it helped to arouse your curiosity."

Shaun felt his mouth go dry. "If all this is really happening," he said, "there has to be a reason."

"Oh, it's happening all right, Shaun, and there is a reason."

"Then I need to know it – now!" snapped Shaun, feeling far less brave than he hoped he sounded.

"What would you say," Jarrod continued, "if I were to tell you that everything that's happened to you since you left the excavation site has taken place within one minute?" He paused for Shaun's reaction.

"What are you talking about?"

"Would it be any more 'unreal' than anything else that's happened so far?" went on Jarrod.

"That's just it, mister..."

"Jarrod, please."

Shaun ignored the interruption. "That's just it – I'm not sure what *has* happened so far."

"Let me explain. Imagine being able to control a period of time so that it can be 'lengthened' to allow more happenings to take place within it – a 'time-stretch' – or being able to 'shorten' it so that a whole day can go by in a split-second; what you might call a 'time-squash'."

"I don't know what you're talking about," said Shaun.

Jarrod rose and paced the room. "Of course you don't," he said, "it'd be unreasonable to expect you to, there are people on my own planet who don't..."

"Planet! Did you say 'planet'?"

Jarrod soft-pedalled. "In another solar system, the planet Grava."

Shaun took a step backwards. "Look mister ... Jarrod ... whatever your name is, I don't know what I'm doing here, I don't even know why I'm here, but whatever it is you want..."

"Please," cut in Jarrod, then again, pleading, "please, you won't be harmed. Please just ... listen."

"I think I've heard enough."

"Just five minutes, give me five minutes, that's all I ask."

Shaun eyed him warily.

Jarrod indicated the chair again, and after a long pause, Shaun sidled into it.

"As I was saying," Jarrod continued, "it may seem like a while to you, an hour, maybe, but in real terms, in Earth terms, it has been just one minute since you left the archaeological site to go home."

Shaun eyed him, disbelief and distrust written all over his face.

"What time did you leave?"

"What?"

"What time did you leave the site?"

"Er . . . ten to seven."

"Have you looked at your watch since?"

"No."

"Look at it now."

Shaun looked. It was nine minutes to seven, and the second hand wasn't moving. He shook his wrist, then listened. "It's stopped. . ." he began, then swallowed hard.

Jarrod resumed his seat and waited for Shaun's attention to focus on him once more. "People caught up in these 'time-styles' might have the impression that time is normal . . . like you. Since you left the site, you, Shaun, have been in a time-stretch."

Shaun's thoughts raced. Even if all that Jarrod told him was true (and he was beginning to get a very uncomfortable feeling that it might be) it still left the unanswered question – WHY had he been brought here?

"Because we need your help," said Jarrod.

Shaun shook his head. "Me? *You* need my help? With all this? I don't see it. . ."

"Don't underestimate yourself, Shaun," said Jarrod. "You are important to us." He swung in his chair, pressed a couple of buttons, and at once the facing wall came alive with moving pictures. "This," he said with obvious pride, "is Grava."

Choosing his words carefully, Jarrod drew Shaun a picture of the situation existing on his home planet. Shaun listened, in disbelief at first, but gradually the story, detailed as it was, told with such sincerity, began to seep through to him. What he was being told, however unlikely, *had* to be true. No one would go to all this trouble to lie.

"Unless we act quickly," Jarrod continued, "and unless you help us, Grava will become utterly depopulated."

There was a silence, broken only by the buzzing and clicking of the surrounding machinery.

"I still don't see how. . ." said Shaun. "I mean, a disease . . . wouldn't you be better with a doctor, or something?"

Jarrod paused before replying. The hesitation lent emphasis to his words. "You can save us," he replied, simply. "We won't force you to do anything." He paused. "But we *hope* you will want to."

Shaun felt a crushing wave of responsibility sweep over him. What was it they wanted him to do? What if he couldn't? What if he was incapable of helping? What then?

"A cure for the disease exists," Jarrod said, "in the year 894 AD." He took a deep breath and exhaled. "We need you to go back and retrieve it," he said, evenly.

At first, Shaun thought he might have misheard. Jarrod's next words told him he hadn't.

"You're the only one who can do it."

"I don't understand," stammered Shaun. "Why me? Why can't it be one of you? Why anybody? Can't it just be ... I don't know ... 'transported' or whatever?"

"Not that easy, Shaun," said Jarrod. The door had slid silently open, and Silak Tulkan had slid, almost as silently, in. The sight of him aroused fresh suspicions in Shaun, and for the first time, he felt glad that Jarrod was in the room also.

Jarrod introduced Tulkan with a tone to his voice that was not lost on Shaun. The newcomer was obviously not the blond man's favourite person, and what made it all the more chilling was that Tulkan appeared not to be aware of it – though Shaun was sure that he must be.

"Tulkan will explain the theory behind the retrieval," Jarrod said.

Tulkan took up a position against the wall, his arms

folded, his arrogant nose held high as he peered over it. "Inanimate objects, such as the phial which contains the cure," he began, "can only travel through time in the possession of a person or animal. Furthermore, living things can only be transported through time by what we know as C.A.M. – 'Chromosome Alignment Method'. This is where transportation waves are locked on to chromosome patterns of inheritance shared equally between two people, one here and one in the past."

"Inheritance?" said Shaun. "You mean ... some distant relative?"

Jarrod nodded. "You see, Shaun, not only do we know exactly where the Phial is right now, we know exactly who has it."

Shaun hesitated before asking. "Who?"

"Your direct ancestor," put in Tulkan. "He is the link we need to transport you back to the Year of the Phial. The year 894 AD."

There was silence for a long time, broken eventually by Jarrod. "So now you know," he said. "And what *we* need to know is, will you do it?"

Shaun's head swam with the enormity of it all. Any minute now, he just knew, he was going to wake up in bed and find he'd been dreaming the lot!

Jarrod rose and paced to the other side of the room, then turned and paced slowly back again.

"Take your time, Shaun," he said, "and bear in mind that there could be dangers."

"What Commander Jarrod means, Shaun," cut in Tulkan, hastily, "is that dangers do exist, naturally, as with most things in life, but we have absolute control over events, and risks of anything going wrong, well, are virtually non-existent..."

Jarrod eased some menace into his voice. "I will not have the boy going under any false illusions, Tulkan. He deserves to know the risks!"

"Risks!" laughed Tulkan. "Really!"

"No one will blame you if you say 'no', Shaun," said Jarrod. "You've nothing to prove." And he glared at Tulkan.

"Would I have to go alone?"

Tulkan drew his eyes from Jarrod's to answer Shaun: "Two people of similar density *could* be transported together, but it would reduce the efficiency of the transport mechanism. We'd have to find somebody with the same height and weight – and time's against us. This mission is too important to risk failure due to overloading."

"What about getting back?" asked Shaun, tentatively.

"A simple reversal."

"*In theory,*" added Jarrod, ignoring Tulkan's scowl.

For what seemed an age, but what must have been, in reality, only minutes, Shaun contemplated the most difficult decision of his young life. He felt a twinge of conscience as, through the gravity of the situation, came stealing the thought (such a selfish thought) that here was an opportunity to experience what life would actually have been like in the Anglo-Saxon days.

Was this an opportunity he could afford to miss? He pushed the thought from his mind; that was not the reason he would be going – if he chose to go.

And if he didn't? If he didn't, if he refused, then, if Jarrod was to be believed, a whole civilization would be wiped out. Millions and millions of people would die, people whom he might have been able to save.

Of course there would be risks, and Jarrod at least was trying to be honest about them, but there were risks in crossing the road, never mind crossing a few hundred years. Again the longing came upon him to know what life had been like then; it was all he'd ever *wanted* to know.

The more he pondered, the more he feared that this was a challenge that it might be in his nature to take up – and that bothered him.

Tulkan bothered him also; he didn't like the man.

He turned to Jarrod. "If I go – *if* – and I'm not saying I will, can I be brought back at any time, whether I have this Phial or not?"

"Absolutely," cut in Tulkan.

Shaun looked to Jarrod for the answer, and Jarrod nodded. Shaun drew a deep breath, exhaled slowly, and shook his head. "I don't know," he said. "I just don't know."

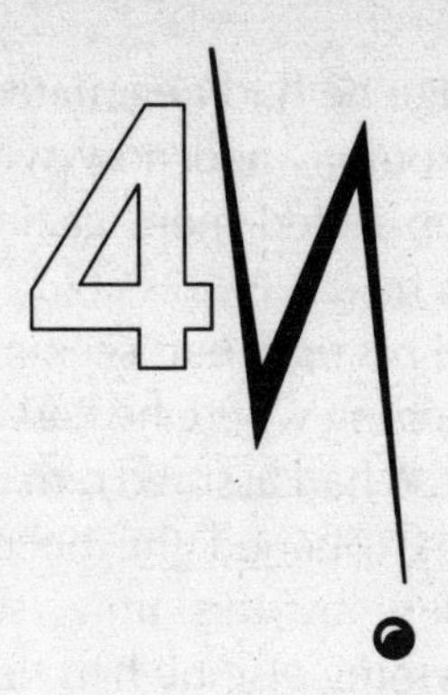

Mission

Jarrod stood, framed in the doorway of the time-transfer capsule in the heart of the silvery pod which Shaun had seen on his arrival at the cavern. He pocketed the wrist watch that Shaun handed to him.

Shaun sat centrally in the cornerless chamber, hands clasping kneecaps, heart pounding like a sledgehammer. A row of lights that stretched around the room winked in sequence through the whole colour spectrum. He was nervous, and apprehensive, sure of only one thing, and that was his uncertainty. Even now, as he was about to be projected, he could hardly believe that he had agreed to undertake this mission, and yet there was one small part of him that rejoiced at the thought of what was about to happen.

Through the doorway, over Jarrod's shoulder, he

could see the ledge he had negotiated on his way to Jarrod's control room, lined now with men, intent, anxious-faced, zip-suited men, gazing down at the capsule in which he sat.

Shaun fingered his right ear, seeking out the bump just inside the opening where he had allowed Tulkan to inject him. Jarrod had assured him it would be OK, and Tulkan had explained the necessity for it, an explanation which, by this time, seemed no less unlikely than anything else he had heard. The bump was an implant which, he was told, would act as a translator and allow him to understand the Old English dialect he could expect to hear from the people he would be dealing with. It would also enable him to be understood when he spoke.

What next, he thought? A stun phaser like the ones on Star Trek? How had he got himself into this position?

"You'll feel nothing," Jarrod said, startling him. "Try to relax. We do know how to control all this."

Shaun managed a faint smile, and glanced at his empty wrist, anxious to curtail the waiting.

"You left the dig two minutes ago," Jarrod said. "We can *suspend* time if we have to. We have the capability, at least, to create that illusion."

"For me?" asked Shaun. "Or the people here?"

"There is someone expecting you, at home?"

"My parents."

"If everything goes to plan, they won't even know

you've been delayed." Jarrod stepped into the capsule, and crouched down, saying, "Listen. While you're away, we can neither see nor hear you. You'll appear on our screens as a red dot – so will the Phial. When you pick up the Phial, the dots converge. That's when we bring you back."

Shaun listened carefully, knowing his life probably depended on how well he understood the situation.

"We can monitor your condition. We'll know if you're asleep or awake, ill, or in danger. We can recall you instantly."

"How will you know the extent of the danger if I can't be seen?"

"A good question," said Jarrod. "Here's the answer." He held out his hand; nestling in his palm was a small, red, oval disc. "Take it."

Shaun did so.

"We can bring you back any time, and we will if we think it's necessary, but only you know exactly what's going on. This disc is activated by your thought patterns, or at least, those thought patterns which carry a strong enough instruction. If you need to get out quickly, hold it in your palm, and make the decision to leave as strongly as you can in your mind."

Here Shaun would have interrupted, but Jarrod held up a silencing hand. He spoke slowly, purposefully. "It must be a moment of total commitment.

Don't doubt your decision. Above all, don't change your mind. Do you understand?"

Shaun nodded.

"If you commit yourself to return," Jarrod whispered, "you're like an arrow to its target; a good marksman needs commitment, concentration." He smiled, held out his hand. "Good luck, Shaun," he said, "and thanks." And turning, he stepped outside the door.

The door clicked smoothly into place, and the only thing to show that there had ever been a door there was the gap in the row of winking lights.

Shaun swallowed hard, already regretting the decision he'd made. For a minute or so nothing happened, then, slowly at first, the lights began to increase their speed. He watched as first one colour, then another, seemed to dominate. Red quickly gave way to orange, then yellow took over, the colours magnified by the silky-smoothness of the walls.

Green. Getting faster all the time, becoming a blur as blue predominated. He became aware of a thin, high-pitched whistle as blue ghosted into indigo.

Violet! The capsule filled with an unearthly violet light which lasted only seconds before giving way to the purest white he had ever seen. The whistle, which had been climbing steadily, note by note, cut out abruptly, then. . .

There was darkness, cold, and a breeze was blowing on his cheek. After the brilliance of the white light, it took some seconds to accustom his eyes to the blackness all around him. The first things he saw were stars, and he realized that he was lying on his back looking up at the night sky. The capsule he had been in a moment ago was nowhere to be seen.

He rolled to his left, and drew a sharp breath – there, lying next to him, was a dead man, a gash across his face, eyes staring, tunic soaked in blood. Instinctively he rolled away, trying to scramble to his feet, but only succeeded in stumbling over another mutilated body to his right. Panting, he dropped to his knees, and found himself looking at the legs of someone standing over him. The legs were apart, and braced for action.

Shaun looked up, and his heart almost stopped. The figure had a huge sword held aloft in both hands, ready to strike.

Paralysed with horror, he heard, as if in a nightmare, the cry of anger, and watched as the moonlight glinted wickedly on the descending blade.

Rolf

All day the sound of battle had drifted from the bay. Rolf straightened from the whetstone on which he was sharpening his dagger, pushed the copper-red hair from his eyes, and swept his gaze over the rim of the hill.

He listened, aware that around him others were doing the same. No sound broke the stillness, and the villagers knew that the battle was over. Rolf rammed his dagger angrily into his belt, the frustration he had felt all day boiling over. When the news had come from the lookouts early that morning that the Viking longboats had been sighted, he had been amongst the first to arm himself. An attack had been expected; many Saxon villages along the coast had suffered lately at the hands of the invaders, and Rolf had been ready and eager to stand shoulder to shoulder with the village men to fight for the community. But he knew his father, Oswold, the village leader, would choose him, and most of the other younger men, to remain and protect the village; to be "rearguard".

It was tradition, the Saxon way of ensuring that there were always enough young men left to provide the next generation, but such a move never failed to promote bitter disappointment amongst those left behind, who wanted nothing more than to show their worth.

He had waited until the men were leaving to meet the enemy on the beach, before slipping in amongst them. It had been his uncle who had spotted him and sent him back to the village with his ears ringing.

Right now, with the battle seemingly over, it occurred to him that the edge he had just put on his dagger might yet be put to use.

Very soon now there would be figures coming over the hill, and depending upon how the battle had gone, they could either be returning Saxons or, gods forbid, victorious Vikings coming to plunder the village.

Even as he watched, the outline of the hill rippled and broke as a number of men scrambled over and began to make their way down to the scattering of Saxon dwellings. Those watching held their breath, unable to tell from this distance if the figures were friends or foe, then, as the approaching men neared, slithering and winding their way between the trees on the slope, a cheer of recognition went up from the watching group, and Rolf's tense muscles relaxed.

Minutes later, the first of the battle-weary Saxons staggered into the camp, supported by those of his family who had rushed out to meet him. All around, women and children were running out to aid the returning fighters, searching amongst them for faces they knew.

Rolf's mother came from their hut and stood with him, quietly waiting, watching. Neither she nor Rolf would have any difficulty in spotting Oswold, even from a distance; his tall, muscular frame was distinctive, and the red hair was like a beacon. When they did spot him, then would be the time to run to him, tend to his wounds. They waited until the main body of warriors had returned, many carrying or supporting an injured comrade.

Oswold was not amongst them.

Neither was he one of those who followed later, delayed by more serious injury, and as the flow of men slowed to a trickle, Rolf placed an arm tenderly around his mother's shoulders, his heart heavy, tears burning the back of his eyes.

The day was ending as the last of the survivors arrived, and though Rolf and his mother continued to stare up the slope, willing the figure of Oswold to appear, they both knew that it was a futile hope.

* * *

The fires burned brightly that night, and around each one the villagers huddled, listening to the tales of bravery from those able and willing to tell of the battle. It had indeed been a fierce fight, and one which could have gone either way had not Oswold rallied his men at one particular stage of the battle and literally forced the Vikings back to their boats and out to sea.

Rolf went from group to group enquiring of his father. It seemed that no one had seen him fall; one minute he was fighting like a wild man, the next he was gone.

It was later that night, when the fires had all burned low, and Rolf's mother had sobbed herself to sleep, that Rolf rose and crept silently from the hut.

The moon was high, lighting the way as he strode from the village and began to climb the slope up which so many good men had marched that morning, and which had seen many fewer return.

It was Saxon custom that those who died in battle were left to rest on the battlefield until the following dawn before their bodies were removed for burial, and strictly speaking, no one was allowed to disturb the battlefield until then.

But Rolf couldn't bear to think of his father lying out there on his own, and though he was, in every respect, a true Saxon, he could see no sense in a custom which prevented him from being with the father he loved, dead though he might be.

He was taking such care that no one from the village saw him climb the hill, that he was taken by surprise at the sudden attack. An arm reached out as he passed a tree, a strong hand covered his mouth, stifling the grunt of surprise, and he felt the cold metal of the dagger pressed against his throat.

His reactions were instinctive.

Grasping the wrist of the dagger-hand, he heaved and shifted his body, so that the weight of his attacker became a weapon in his own favour, and toppled him, head first, over his shoulder to land with a thud on the ground. Rolf's own dagger leapt to his hand as he readied himself to face his assailant.

"Dirk!"

By the light of the moon, there was no mistaking the broad features and dark mop of hair that belonged to his best friend.

"You fool! I nearly killed you!"

Dirk climbed slowly to his feet, dusting his tunic.

"*You* nearly killed *me*? Whose dagger was at whose throat?"

"You must have known it was me. The moon is bright enough."

"A test of your reactions." Dirk's face clouded, his tone became more solemn. "I heard about your father; I knew you would be coming this way."

"Let's hope no one else did." Rolf paused, then said, "Did you lose someone today?"

Dirk nodded. "Edgar, my cousin," he scowled

fiercely. "Put just one dog of a Dane within my sword's length..."

Rolf clapped a hand on his friend's shoulder. "They will *all* be avenged, Dirk, have no fear of that."

He turned, and continued his trudge up the hill. Dirk sheathed his dagger and followed him, as he had done since they were both old enough to walk. Their respect for each other was complete and unquestionable, and they shared a loyalty that had blossomed, over the years, into true friendship, a friendship that made them a team, and closer almost than brothers.

Nothing could have prepared them for the sight that met their eyes as they topped the ridge and looked down on that scene of human destruction. It was a small bay, but even so, from the foot of the hill to the sea there was hardly a patch of sand showing between the bodies which lay there, silent in death, the body armour and discarded weapons throwing back glints of moonlight.

But it was not the sight of the carnage which caught their immediate attention. At one end of the bay, gleaming dully, was a large, perfectly circular object.

If either of them had known the word, they would have described it as "hovering"; all they knew was that it was most definitely not resting on the beach. It gave off no noise, just hung there, a bright, iridescent green, for all the world like a huge, round shield, domed at the centre as a shield would be, the dome emblazoned with letters and numbers, meaningless to the two onlookers, but reading DX900. Its underside pulsed with light, first one colour, then another, continuously: red, orange, yellow, green, blue, over and over in rapid sequence.

They stared, open-mouthed, and shared a glance of incredulity. Dirk's face sagged in disbelief as he struggled to find a voice.

"What . . . is it?" he croaked.

But a shocked Rolf had no answer.

Then, as they watched, the chromatic pattern of lights changed, the blue held, intensifying, before ghosting to a pure, pure white, and the object began to move, skimming the beach and the bodies on it towards the other end of the bay.

Captain Dol Arit of the probe ship Quatar gazed dolefully at the scene of carnage that his monitors were showing him, as the ship passed slowly over the bay. His instruments had given no indication of life-signs, but he had been obliged, nonetheless, to obey Council rules and to exit the ship, accompanied by his chief medical officer, to confirm this.

Now, back aboard, all that remained was to allow the sensors to count the bodies as the ship passed over them, and to enter the incident in the memory bank. His face told its own story as he viewed the waste of human life.

A bleep from the console told him that the count

had been completed and logged, and he turned to his first officer.

"Forward away," he said, grimly. "Take us out of this area."

Rolf and Dirk gaped as the huge object lifted, showing its flat, smooth underside, and shot, with the speed of an arrow from a well-flexed bow, up into the night sky. Within the space of two heartbeats it became as small as one of the stars above their heads, then almost disappeared altogether, but as they stared, the speck of light grew larger once again.

"It returns!" breathed Dirk.

The chief medical officer aboard the Quatar was apologetic.

"The phial must have slipped from my belt," he said to his captain.

Captain Arit brushed aside his concerns. "No matter, doctor," he assured him, "it will take only moments to retrieve it."

The navigator's procedure was simple enough; all he had to do was engage reverse polarity, and as he did so, the ship immediately began its return to the surface. It was his next act that brought about the disaster. It had been a long journey, and the navigator was at the end of a long shift, he was tired. Instead of confirming the reverse movement, an act designed to boost the reactors and speed the ship on its way, he punched in "forward thrust". The opposing forces literally ripped the DX900 apart.

Rolf and Dirk saw the flash, followed a moment or two later by a muffled bang, and the object they were watching simply ceased to exist.

For a long time they said nothing, willing their minds to accept what they had just witnessed; all else, even the butchery below, for the moment forgotten. When they did speak, it was with the half-hope that each would be able to confirm the other's sighting, and in doing so, confirm each other's sanity.

Rolf spoke first. "What I saw ... you saw?"

Dirk nodded dumbly, swallowed over a dry throat. "We must warn the village," he muttered.

"Of what?"

"Of what we saw!"

"And what *did* we see?"

"It flew! Like a bird, it flew!"

"Without wings?"

"I saw none."

"And they will believe this, the villagers? That something so big, so bright, without wings, or head, or tail – flew, *that* fast?"

Dirk hesitated.

"We would be laughed from the village!" Rolf went on, "No, Dirk, what we saw we cannot tell. No one would believe. I *saw* it, and *I* don't believe!"

For long minutes they sat, re-living the experience,

unable to call upon anything within their understanding which might give a glimmer of explanation.

"But what was it?" mumbled Dirk for the tenth time.

"Something . . . something we were not meant to see. Something not of this land."

"Then it must have been of the devil!" whispered Dirk. "All this death, all this destruction; it was the devil, claiming his own!"

Rolf nodded slowly. "Maybe. . ." he murmured, "maybe. . ."

The moon was beginning to wane before they finally made a move for the beach, subdued by the grimness of the task that lay ahead of them – the need to view each Saxon body in the hope of identifying Rolf's father and Dirk's cousin.

The sighting of the probe ship was still heavy on their minds as they reached the first of the corpses, and slowly edged their way along, peering at each. They recognized more than one neighbour, more than one friend. Dirk's cousin, Edgar, lay surrounded by dead Vikings, having sold his life dearly, but nowhere did they see the body of Oswold.

Unwittingly, they eventually found themselves in the area in which they had first spotted the probe ship, and it was there that a dull glint, different from the glimmer of a weapon, caught Rolf's eye. Stooping, he picked the object up to see that it was a slim, round-ended cylinder about the length of his hand, light, and silky smooth to the touch. Around its middle was a single red stripe.

Intrigued, he tucked it into his belt pouch and continued the grim search.

Step by step, body by body, the two friends picked their way over the beach, stopping from time to time to check, with a shrug or a shake of the head, that neither had found the one person they were looking for, and as they neared the far rocks that marked the end of the battlefield, a strange hope arose in Rolf that his father's body would not be there at all.

Which introduced one possibility: it was not unknown for the Vikings to take prisoners, even in retreat.

Could his father have been loaded on to a long-boat, possibly wounded and unconscious, and taken away?

Oswold's stature, his fierceness and his unquestionable leadership would have singled him out as a worthwhile hostage.

Eventually, Rolf and Dirk found themselves with one final group of bodies to investigate.

They approached, and saw with relief that none of the three Saxon warriors that lay there was Oswold.

They had covered the whole battlefield, stared into the face of each and every dead villager, and seen that Oswold was not amongst them.

They clasped each other in relief.

The prospect of his father as a prisoner was much

more acceptable to Rolf than the thought of his death; now there was hope, something to plan around, and he knew he could never rest until his father's release from captivity had been achieved.

Then a movement caught his eye; Dirk saw it at the same time. A youth, he looked to be about their age, with copper-red hair like himself, was lying between two of the bodies they had just examined.

But how?

He had not been there a moment before, they would swear to it! And his clothing – so odd. As they stared, bewildered, the boy rolled, gave a cry of alarm as he came upon the body to his left, scrambled away, stumbled, and fell to his knees in front of Dirk.

In his search, Dirk had retrieved the sword that had belonged to his cousin, and as the boy knelt before him, Dirk raised the sword above his head.

Whoever this stranger was, nothing about him was Saxon, neither his clothing nor his manner, therefore he must be Dane, a Viking, an enemy, one responsible for the death of Edgar, for the loss of all the good Saxon villagers he'd seen this night.

With a cry of anger, Dirk brought the sword flashing down, its keen edge aimed at the youth's skull.

Realization

"No!"

Without fully knowing why, Rolf launched himself in a shoulder charge at his friend. It was like hitting a brick wall, but, coming from an unexpected quarter, it was enough to spoil Dirk's aim, and the swordpoint cut a neat slit in the material covering the boy's upper arm on its way to the ground.

Rolf placed himself between the stranger and Dirk, whose look of surprise was quickly turning to anger. Then the anger on Dirk's face melted into wonderment.

The stranger had risen to his feet, and was looking over Rolf's shoulder at his muscular attacker. For the second time that night, Dirk's jaw dropped as he saw the distinct resemblance between the youth and Rolf.

Rolf turned, and drew breath sharply as the similarity hit him, too. The nose was broader, the eyes a darker blue, Rolf's face was more lean, but the same copper redness in the hair was there, worn shorter by the stranger, but the exact same colour.

For his part, Shaun was no less awed. He hadn't known quite what to expect upon his arrival, and in the rush of everything, the last thing he had given any thought to was the person from whom he might receive the Phial. He had understood that it would be a direct ancestor, but suddenly to find himself face to face with that person, and to find that they shared so many similarities of appearance, was almost too much to take in at one go.

Rolf and Shaun held each other's gaze for a long moment, Dirk hovering suspiciously in the background, sword ever ready, then Rolf cautiously reached out a hand and, as though to assure himself that what he saw was real, touched Shaun's cheek, ran a finger of bewilderment over his nose, and felt the texture of his hair.

"Who are you?" he breathed. "So like me, and yet not?"

Shaun swallowed, his tongue dry. The words, obviously spoken in Old English, formed into perfect speech in his head, and instinctively he scrabbled mentally for a reply, hastily throwing together the makings of an answer from what he knew of the language. Any faith he had in the translator implant disappeared like a wisp of smoke, despite what he was hearing. He was suddenly aware that when he did speak, he would be speaking *directly* to his own ancestor.

"I am Shaun," he said, eventually, and from their faces he could tell that, though his accent might be strange to them, they understood.

"Shaun," echoed Rolf. Shaun nodded.

"And why do I feel I know you . . . Shaun?"

"Because. . ." Shaun tried desperately to think of a simple explanation, ". . .because we have the same family."

"He lies!" spat Dirk. "You would have known of this. Listen to his speech! He is a traitor, a spy for the Vikings!"

Rolf raised a hand to silence his friend. "How come you here, and why so strange a clothing?"

"There's a lot I need to explain. . ."

"Explain then," put in Dirk, "before my sword makes it difficult to do so."

Rolf threw a sharp glance at Dirk. "We will hear what he has to say . . . come." And turning, he led the way to the hill fringing the sand.

Shaun followed, thankful of the time to gather his thoughts and to sort out his reasoning, to familiarize himself with the phrases he was likely to need. The wary Dirk brought up the rear as they wound a path over the body-strewn beach to the foot of the hill.

With barely a hesitation, Rolf led the way up the

slope and on to the flat dusty area at the top, where he indicated to Shaun that he should sit.

Every step of the way, Shaun had been desperately trying to work out what he was to tell them.

How could he expect them to believe that he was from a thousand years in the future, or that he was Rolf's descendant? Did he even have to? Would it be simpler just to make something up?

He sat, and the others sat facing him.

The big one with the sword and the scowl was going to be particularly hard to convince.

"You say we have the same family..." prompted Rolf.

"In a way..." said Shaun. "I mean, well, yes ... yes, we have."

"I am Rolf, son of Oswold."

Shaun's heart leapt. If he had needed any confirmation, this was it. However, Rolf's next words were less than helpful. "My father," he said, "has neither brother nor sister."

Dirk tapped the sword ominously against a stone. The "family" connection was looking less and less likely.

"I *am* telling you the truth," said Shaun.

"This I hope. It will be hard to kill a traitor with my face."

Shaun's brain raced. Where could he start?

"I ... I have travelled a long distance..." he began.

"But you are not weary, these clothes are not the clothes of a traveller, they have no travel stains."

"Where I live ... travel is different." He took a breath, hitting the difficult part. "We can travel really fast – as ... as fast as ... as fast as a speeding arrow."

"Paahh!" growled Dirk, scornfully.

"Remember how quickly I appeared ... on the sand ... just like that?" He snapped his fingers. "Remember?"

"You were hiding!" retorted Dirk.

"I think not," Rolf said.

"What? He *must* have been..."

"Think on what we also saw tonight, Dirk, that too travelled faster than anything we have seen. As fast as ..." and he tried, unsuccessfully, to repeat Shaun's finger-snapping. "There is more happening on this beach tonight than we know of."

"Or wish to know of," muttered Dirk, darkly.

"I'm just not from *here* – not from this *time*..." They looked at him warily. "If you see what I mean," stuttered Shaun, half to himself.

They didn't see what he meant.

"This 'time'?" said Rolf.

"Yes," said Shaun, "I'll try to explain better ... your 'time' is now, understand? You were born, you'll live, and then ... and then you'll die like everybody has to."

"Some sooner than others," muttered Dirk, his scowl deepening.

Rolf nodded *his* understanding, trying to see the point of what was being said to him so haltingly.

"Well," said Shaun, one eye on the sceptical Dirk, "well . . . *my* time has not yet . . . happened."

Blank stares, but at least they were listening. He went on. "See . . . you are the son of your father, he was the son of *his* father, and so on, back through time, yes?"

They nodded dumbly.

"Your children will have children, and then *they* will have children, right?"

No response.

"They will live in a *different* time, and things in *that* time will be different . . . like travel, that will be different. Well . . . I'm from that time – a time where things are different – a time that has yet to come."

The silence could almost be felt.

Dirk sought Rolf's eyes and held them. "Shall I kill him or shall you?" he said.

Rolf said nothing as Dirk's hand went slowly for the sword. Shaun thought fast. The Phial! Rolf must have the Phial, or know of it at least!

"You have an object," he babbled, desperately, "like this. . ." and he drew with a stick in the dust. "There is a . . . a band around it, here, a red band." He bit his lip, anxious now.

Rolf looked keenly at him.

"This is the reason I'm here. You *must* have it."

Silently, still staring at Shaun, Rolf took the burnished cylinder from his pouch, held it in the palm of his hand.

Shaun eyed it. All he had to do was hold it, even snatch it from Rolf, and in an instant he would be out of this terrible predicament and home safe.

Rolf curled his hand around the Phial, held it tightly, and Shaun's momentary chance had gone.

Dirk sat back, bewildered. "How did he know of that?"

"I found this on the beach at the beginning of our search," explained Rolf. "He could not know – unless he is telling us truth after all."

"Unless he was hiding and *saw* you find it!" snapped Dirk.

Shaun pushed his advantage. "My clothes – look, feel – is that a cloth you've seen before?" He took his tie off. "These colours . . . look!"

A doubt began to creep over their faces, and the look encouraged Shaun; a ray of hope shone. He whipped off his Reeboks, showed them the machine stitching, the logos. If only he hadn't had to leave his watch!

Rolf and Dirk were becoming more interested, and Shaun hoped against hope that that meant more convinced, too.

He emptied his pockets – some string, a pencil, a credit card – intriguing, but useless as proof of his claims – a membership card for the local Archaeological Society, nothing very convincing, and then, from the folds of a hanky dropped a coin, a fifty-pence piece.

Shaun grabbed it eagerly, flourished it, showed the date, 1995, before realizing with a groan that the figures meant nothing to either of them.

It was then that Rolf spotted the membership card; he reached out and picked it up, studying the front cover. His eyes on Shaun, he handed it to Dirk who looked it over similarly, before handing it back.

Slowly, Rolf reached for his dagger.

Shaun feared the worst, and remembering the escape disc that Jarrod had given him, reached into his trouser pocket and gripped it, ready to wish himself away at the slightest hint of aggression.

Rolf reversed the dagger and showed the hilt. On it, carved roughly, was a replica of a crest.

It consisted of a double headed axe, over an owl, within a circle.

Next to the dagger, Rolf laid the membership card, and clearly, above the name of the Society, was the same crest.

"The emblem of our village, Roofwood," said Rolf.

Shaun blinked. Roofwood? Rufford? Could they be the same? Could it be that he was not only conversing with his ancestor, but sitting in the very spot from which his town had originated, a Saxon village called Roofwood? The same village which he was presently helping to excavate?

Rolf, and Dirk too, were now looking at him through slightly different eyes.

"Tell me your family name," said Rolf.

"Oswoldson" he tried to say, but the implant made it come out as "Oswoldbearn".

"Shaun, son of Oswold," muttered Rolf, and held out a hand in friendship. "Welcome."

Decision

For the next two hours, until the first streaks of dawn began to appear in the sky, the three sat and talked, or rather, Shaun talked. Rolf and Dirk were keen listeners, fascinated by Shaun's tale.

Despite Jarrod's efforts in outlining the nature of the time stretch that he was in, Shaun was conscious of the minutes ticking by, but felt that he owed them an explanation. It was the least he could do.

What would a second or two matter? This was his *ancestor* he was talking to; the Phial was safe in Rolf's belt-pouch, and he wanted to remember this incredible moment.

He outlined events to them as simply as he knew how, but there was no doubting that they weren't able to comprehend all that he had to say, and Shaun thought it wise to skirt the issue of Jarrod and the problem on Grava. But he found, to his relief, that he was able to get across the basic concepts behind the reason for him being there, and was impressed by the depth of understanding that Rolf showed, and his willingness to understand. Remembering how he himself had felt when Jarrod had been doing the explaining, helped him to tell the story more convincingly, and at a pace with which they could cope.

Rolf was chiefly intrigued by the fact that Shaun was his descendant, and the rapport and friendship that sprang up between them in that short time was a phenomenon in itself.

The inevitable question eventually came:

"How will you return to your time?" asked Rolf. "And when will you go?"

Shaun looked hard at Rolf and at Dirk. Were they ready for this? Had they already been asked to believe enough for one night?

Rolf seemed to sense his hesitancy. "If it is difficult for you to tell us. . ."

"No . . . no," said Shaun, "you have to know, it's just so. . ." he took a breath, released it. "The object you have," he said, "the Phial, I just have to hold on to it . . . that's all."

"And then?"

"And then I will be gone," said Shaun. "Just like that." He snapped his fingers again.

Dirk gaped, and muttered uneasily under his breath.

Rolf became thoughtful. "What would you do, Shaun, if I did not let you have the Phial?"

Shaun eyed him; did he mean it? "You must," he said. "I told you, the people of ... of *my* time need what's inside, it'll save a lot of lives."

Rolf brought the Phial from his pouch again and studied it closely. "So powerful a thing. If only it was so simple to solve the problems of our people here. Maybe then we could find my father..." he looked at Shaun "...*our* father, and save him from a life of slavery."

Perhaps Rolf was probing for evidence that Shaun cared what happened to Oswold. Perhaps he was feeling as Shaun did, that he should share as much as he could in the precious moments they had together. Shaun appeared to have told him everything; what had he to divulge apart from news of the family they were both a part of?

"You'll find him, I know you will," Shaun said, simply, and hoped with all his heart, as he said it, that Rolf would.

"Yes, in time," Rolf smiled at the pun, "but then, maybe not 'in time'. Maybe he will die before I reach him. Oswold will not sit well in captivity; the Vikings may consider him less trouble dead."

Shaun felt a twinge of guilt, and realized he'd been so bound up in his own problems he hadn't shown much interest in Oswold's predicament. Or in Oswold for that matter. The guilt mingled with anxiety.

In a few minutes he would be gone, and he'd learned nothing of his ancestors or of the life in this age; the once-in-a-lifetime opportunity he'd grasped so eagerly had been virtually wasted. True, he reminded himself, that was not the reason he had agreed to make the journey, but he would never find himself in this position again. And Rolf obviously wanted to talk.

"Your father, do you. . ." he searched for the word, and settled for a phrase he knew was inadequate, "do you 'get along' with your father?"

The implant apparently knew no equivalent for the phrase, and it came out as spoken.

"Along?" asked Rolf.

"Are you friends? Does he share things with you?"

Rolf gave a small, sad smile. "He is a father to be proud of, a friend to everyone."

"And a great leader," put in Dirk, who had been listening whilst still trying to get the hang of finger-snapping. "With Edward's men behind him, Oswold could drive the Viking Danes from our land. We must find him and release him quickly."

"Edward?" said Shaun in surprise. "King Edward?"

"Who else?" said Dirk.

"King Edward," said Shaun, hesitantly, "had an

Ealdorman called Oswold ... he can't be the same man?"

"Of all the Ealdormen in Sussex and the Wolds," said Rolf, "my father is the King's most trusted."

Shaun felt his scalp tingle.

The Oswold he knew of had been prominent in keeping the Vikings from capturing the South lands; had they done so, England, as it is now, would not exist.

And he was Shaun's *direct* ancestor!

The thought leapt to his mind – what would happen if Oswold were to die in a Viking prison camp? If Rolf and Dirk were unsuccessful in freeing him?

But Oswold's achievements *had* taken place. Did that not mean that his freedom from the Vikings was already assured?

Shaun thought not.

Events which were still to happen could well *not* happen if circumstances of the present were changed. He, Shaun, had changed things simply by being here. Would Rolf and Dirk be, right now, searching for Oswold, might they even have *found* Oswold, if he, Shaun, hadn't turned up?

Had he delayed them? Would that delay prove vital to the freeing of Oswold? Had his presence changed things enough to change the whole of history?

"How will you know where to look for him?" queried Shaun, anxiously.

"There can be but one place," said Rolf. "The Vikings have a great camp in the bay to the north. From there they sail out to attack our villages. There is nowhere else they could keep their prisoners."

"You will get help?"

Rolf shook his head. "To gather enough men would take time we do not have. No, Dirk and I will go, we can travel fast."

Shaun shifted uneasily. Obviously, they didn't know the wider importance of freeing Oswold, of what it would mean to the history of England, the survival of the English language, the survival of the English *people.* The very substance of the people of the country would be changed, the whole racial mix would be different if the Vikings had complete rule, and from his history books he knew that the defence of the South lands, and Oswald's efforts in particular, had prevented that from happening. The move to drive out the Vikings had grown, there was no doubt, directly from the success of King Edward's men, led by Oswold, from around 899 AD.

It didn't take a genius to calculate the implications of Oswold dying in captivity before that date!

Literally millions of people who now lived, himself included, would never have had the chance to be born, by virtue of the fact that their ancestral line had never been established!

He felt a desperate need to help, but how could he? He was committed to his own mission.

His conscience wrestled with itself. Which was more important, the saving of lives on a dying planet, or the preservation of lives threatened by a possible change in history brought about, in all probability, by his own interference with the course of events?

Of course, there was no certainty about it. If there had been, it would have been easier to decide what to do. Oswold may still be freed and live to do the work he was destined to do . . . but was that less likely because of Shaun's interference? Could he afford to take that risk? Could he turn his back on the situation, shrug, and tell himself everything would work itself out?

He licked dry lips. "What do you know of the Vikings?" he asked.

"They are murderous swine. . ." began Dirk.

"No, no. . ." Shaun interrupted ". . .of their tactics, their defence strategies, the layout of their camps?"

They shrugged, not sure what he was leading at.

"I know about the Vikings," he said, "their methods, their strengths, weaknesses . . . how they think, how they work."

"Then tell us, if you think it will help."

"It would take too long . . . you need to be shown . . . I need to be there. . ."

"But you said. . ."

"I know what I said," Shaun interjected, "but . . . oh, God," he turned away, his fists balled, "why does it have to be *me*? Why do I have to make the decision?"

He caught a glimmer in Rolf's eye. "You are saying you want to help us?" Rolf asked.

"I just wish..." stammered Shaun.

"We understand," Rolf said, and laid a hand on Shaun's shoulder.

"But you *don't* understand..." wailed Shaun. "I thought that coming here would be ... well ... as simple as they told me it would be. But it hasn't turned out that way."

"And what has changed that?"

"Oswold. He has to be freed."

"We'll do our best."

"No," continued Shaun, "I mean he *has* to be freed."

"He will be, believe me! Why, we would be trying to do so right now if..."

"...if I hadn't delayed you. That's just the point. You shouldn't be here right now, you should be somewhere else, doing what you should be doing, freeing Oswold. The delay I've caused you could mean the difference between his life and death; you said yourself the Vikings may think him less bother dead."

"It touches me, here," Rolf tapped his own chest, "to think that Oswold means so much to you."

"Oswold means much to a lot of people," Shaun replied.

"The dawn is breaking," put in Dirk. "Soon the villagers will come to collect the dead on the beach."

He took out the Phial and held it on the palm of his hand.

Shaun looked from Rolf, to the Phial, then back again. One small movement would be all that it would take, just to reach out and lift that silky cylinder, and he would be gone, back to his own time, back to his home, back to safety.

He owed it to Jarrod and his people to complete what he'd set out to do, but didn't he owe just as much to his own people to do what he could to safeguard their heritage, their very existence?

And Rolf too, he needed all the help he could get. If it wasn't for Rolf or Oswold, he himself wouldn't be alive! How could he now turn his back on the person responsible for his existence? How could he ever live with himself if he did? How could he live with himself if he got home and found that England was no longer the England he had known – knowing that he could have done something about it?

In that moment of hesitation, he knew what he had to do. He had to be sure that Oswold survived. Jarrod would just have to stretch time a little further.

"Your Phial," prompted Rolf.

Shaun said nothing for a long time.

"Keep it for me, Rolf. When I need it, I'll ask you for it."

Rolf smiled, and tucked the Phial away in his pouch.

"Snap! Snap!" Dirk beamed as the fingers he'd been manipulating finally gave off a sound.

Rolf held out his hand, and Shaun grasped it; Dirk reached over and covered both their hands as they made an unspoken pledge to each other.

From the depths of a nearby bush, a pair of eyes watched them, eyes of such a strange shape and colour that they could not possibly belong to anything from this world.

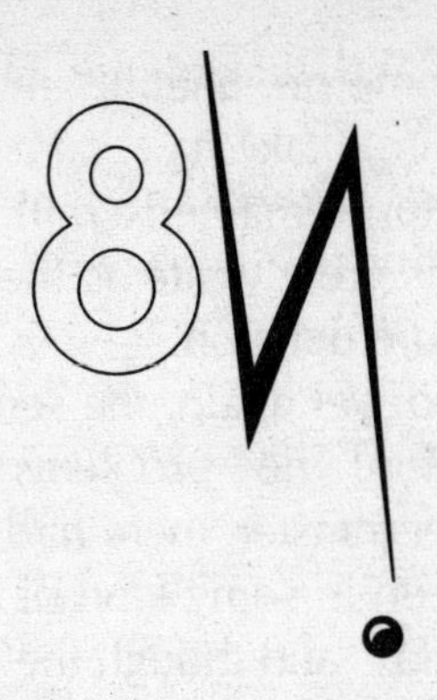

Omnia

In the control room of the centre of operations, Jarrod watched the monitor screens keenly.

The transfer had been a total success, and, thanks to the time-stretch, Shaun had, so far, been gone only twenty seconds of Earth time. The close proximity of the two red dots on the screen told him that contact with the carrier of the Phial had been made, but just what was preventing Shaun from collecting it was impossible to say.

An intense Silak Tulkan hovered like a bird of prey by the Radoforce Impulsator, a piercing, almost mad, light in his eyes, ready on the instant to press the sensorpad which would retrieve both Shaun and the Phial.

"Come on, come on, Shaun," muttered Jarrod to the air around him, "take it . . . *take* it!"

But the indicators remained a millimetre apart, and Tulkan's thin lips grew white as they twisted into a silent sneer of pure derision.

Jarrod checked, yet again, the sensors monitoring Shaun's condition; no problems there. Earlier, immediately after transfer, there *had* been a moment when he had been in some kind of danger, but that had passed quickly, and though the instruments had registered a fairly high stress and anxiety factor since then, it looked now as though his emotions, at least, were functioning normally.

"Your subject seems to be having some kind of problem, Commander Jarrod," hissed Tulkan through clenched teeth, his gimlet eyes glued to the screen. "Perhaps he is not sufficiently motivated?"

Jarrod ignored the barbed remark, knowing that it was intended to discredit Jarrod in the eyes of those present. But what *was* the problem? Why wasn't Shaun making contact with the Phial? Was he, for some reason, unable to? Or did he, as Jarrod was beginning to suspect, have reasons of his own for not doing so?

Jarrod considered himself to be a pretty good judge of character, and the respect and admiration he felt for Shaun led him to believe that, if Shaun had such a reason, then it must be a defendable one.

He was, after all, an Earthling, not a Gravatite. He

couldn't be expected to obey on the instant as a Gravatite would. Earthlings had a series of complex emotions which had to be taken into account, and which tended to affect the decisions they made – feelings, Jarrod was aware, which most Gravatites had once had, but which had been lost to them over the generations.

Long before Jarrod's time, Grava had been populated by people who possessed many of the qualities he had seen in Earthlings over the years: compassion; love; concern; bravery; loyalty; unselfishness; determination. Of course, on the down side, there was the greed, the hate, the violence and the envy, but the very existence of such vices tended to bring out the best in many Earthlings.

But it had all changed: Grava was now an emotionless planet. Its disease-free, leisurely, over-pleasant environment had, for many generations now, failed to give Gravatites problems they might solve, issues they might contest, anxieties and stresses they might grapple with, learn from. The lack of such adversities had not only weakened their spirit, but had gradually, over hundreds of years, bleached all emotion from the race.

It was at times like these, when he saw the potential of the human spirit, that Jarrod grieved that his people had lost the ability to live in anything but a clinical world, where the greatest decision any of them was likely to make was which button to press next.

There were exceptions, however, and Jarrod was one of them.

It was more than ambition that had brought him this far; he was a throwback to the Old Times, one of the few of his race who had inherited not just the potential, but the actuality of emotion. It had given him the edge over his more passive fellow-officers, many of whom saw him as a threat to their own positions because of it.

The Governor knew that Jarrod, unlike the others, was prepared to take risks which sometimes produced results unobtainable by other means, and Jarrod strongly suspected that this was why he had been chosen to head the Phial Retrieval Mission. If only he was given the opportunity, he knew he could sort out Grava's other main problem too – the continuous aggression by their neighbouring planet, Omnia.

From time to time, perhaps fifteen or twenty times each generation, a person was born whose genetic links to the Old Times were so strong that he or she was actually born crying.

These "Cry-borns" invariably grew up with a complete set of emotional responses similar to those known to have existed in all people in the Days of Legend, emotions now termed "Old Values".

Jarrod was one of these. In fact, Jarrod had been born not only crying, but screaming.

Drago, his friend, was another; though Drago's emotion level was less heightened than Jarrod's.

Some Cry-borns learned to control their emotions in an attempt to fit into society; for others, the struggle for control lasted a lifetime; yet others, like Jarrod, rejoiced in their difference, and mourned the fact that their breadth of feeling was denied to the majority of the population.

Tulkan had been a Cry-born, but in his case, one particular emotion, greed, had dominated, and his greed had fed other undesirable emotions in him, like jealousy and a lack of compassion. However, his unusually high level of intelligence had enabled him to conceal his darker side from most people – Jarrod excepted.

"Hardly a difficult manoeuvre, to reach out and pick up an object...!" Tulkan's whining voice brought Jarrod's mind back to sharp focus.

The monitors showed that the red-dot indicators were about to converge; they needed to overlap completely before they could be sure that Shaun had the Phial firmly in his hand. For a long moment the position held, then Jarrod uttered a grunt of frustration and slapped hard on the desk top as the two moved apart. His crew looked sideways at him, raised eyebrows to each other, and Tulkan didn't miss the opportunity to capitalize on the moment by shaking a sad head. The crew had been warned that Jarrod was an intense man, likely to show primitive emotions from time to time; a fault (in their eyes) in an otherwise flawless officer.

An adjutant approached. "Commander Jarrod, the governor of Grava wishes to speak to you."

Jarrod sighed, and nodded his understanding. "Don't take your eyes from your instruments for one instant," he rapped, and so saying, left his seat and walked behind the partition which separated the subspace communications module from the rest of the room.

Tulkan raised a supercilious eyebrow as his only indication that Jarrod's order had been received.

Jarrod's presence brought the holocube into focus, and floating before him suddenly was the figure of the governor of Grava.

"Commander, what news?" asked the governor.

Jarrod made his report, and received in reply the latest grim statistics on the spread of the Sporon disease. In the space of that day, the governor told him, close on one million Gravatites had died, and although this news was more than enough to account for the strain showing on the governor's face, Jarrod sensed that there was even worse news to follow.

He was right.

"Your subject in the Year of the Phial, Commander..."

"The young man, Shaun," Jarrod reminded him.

"...has he many of the Old Values?"

"It would appear so, sir. He certainly possesses

courage and determination. I do not believe he will let us down."

There was a pause.

"He will have need of all his wit, his cunning, *and* his courage," replied the governor.

Jarrod's eyes narrowed. "For any particular reason, sir?" he asked.

"For the worst possible reason, Commander." Another pause. "Our sources confirm that the Omnians are involved."

"In what way?"

"They have sent an agent into the Year of the Phial."

Dirk

Rolf and Shaun sat on a log in the growing light of the new day. Dirk was not with them; he had returned to the village to fetch a more suitable set of clothes for Shaun to wear. As they waited for him, they went over the plan which they hoped would result in Oswold's release from captivity, presuming that he was being held in the Viking's main encampment.

As they talked, they glimpsed Dirk returning, a bundle under his arm. Rolf waved, and Dirk waved back.

Now that he had made the decision to delay his return home, all Shaun's doubts about whether it was the right thing to do had evaporated.

So far on his mission, he had done all that had been

asked of him, and there was no way that anyone could have predicted the circumstances in which he now found himself.

Rolf and Oswold's problem was one that he had to see resolved; one so full of potential disaster that he knew he couldn't afford to leave the outcome to chance.

Rolf looked up, expecting to see Dirk striding towards them, and raised a surprised eyebrow as he saw that he had not yet appeared around the bush they had just seen him approaching. As soon as Shaun had changed into the clothing that Dirk was bringing, the three of them planned to set off north towards the Viking camp. Rolf pointed out to Shaun the two great fells they would have to scale, and he estimated that, if they travelled fast, they would reach the cliffs overlooking the Viking's bay by late afternoon.

Again he glanced towards where he expected Dirk to appear, anxious now to be off. "Dirk!" he called, and then said to Shaun: "The villagers will be here soon, where is he?"

He began to stride over to the bank of bush, but stopped short as his friend emerged.

"Dirk, we must hurry now, come quickly!" and so saying, he returned to stand with Shaun.

Dirk seemed to move incredibly slowly for one who must have known how short of time they were. It was almost as though his legs were suddenly too heavy for him, and he stumbled as he came.

Rolf, eager to be away, didn't notice at first, but Shaun saw that Dirk wore something of a blank expression.

Then Rolf noticed. He looked closely at him and frowned. "Dirk," he said, "are you all right?"

Dirk made no reply, just looked from one to the other of them before nodding, almost as an afterthought.

"Where are the clothes for Shaun?"

For a moment, no longer, a look of alarm came over Dirk's broad face, then, as quickly, he recovered, turned, and lumbered back to the bushes.

Rolf turned to Shaun, concerned. "What's wrong with him?"

"Perhaps the climb up the hill tired him?" suggested Shaun.

Rolf shrugged. "The shock of everything? Maybe he's finding it all hard to accept?"

At that moment, Dirk re-appeared, the bundle of clothes jammed awkwardly under one arm, not carried, just wedged there.

Shaun took them from him, and began to put them on.

"I expect the village is much in mourning," Rolf said, and Dirk nodded. "And your family, they will be mourning Edgar..." He laid a hand on Dirk's shoulder. "Fear not, my friend, our chance for revenge is near. Be not so sad, you know you are with friends."

Dirk cast a glance at Rolf's comforting hand, and put his own hand on Rolf's shoulder, still no flicker of emotion on his face.

"Do you feel well enough to travel with us?" Rolf asked.

"Travel?" said Dirk, as though using that particular word for the first time.

"To the Viking camp... Dirk, what is the matter? Do you wish to stay and be with your family at this time? Is that it? If so, I will understand."

Before Dirk had a chance to reply, a distant babble of voices alerted them to the fact that the villagers were pressing up the hill to claim the bodies from the beach.

"Almost ready," called Shaun, slipping on the leather foot coverings and taking care, last of all, to transfer the oval disc that Jarrod had given him to the pouch around his belt.

"Dirk?" queried Rolf.

A moment, then Dirk nodded. "Let us go," he said.

Rolf turned and loped away along the ridge of the hill, and Shaun jogged after him.

Neither of them saw Dirk's eyes blaze once again with uncertainty as they went, but when next they looked back, Dirk, though a fair distance behind, was moving steadily after them.

They ran for perhaps a mile before Shaun, panting

hard, drew up to where Rolf, his own breathing scarcely ruffled, had stopped to verify the direction in which they were travelling.

Dirk had made up a little ground on them, but was running with an awkwardness which didn't seem to make full use of his rugged frame and sturdy legs. Rolf was still obviously concerned for him and said so.

"I thought he was doing pretty well, actually," wheezed Shaun. "He doesn't look half as tired as I feel."

"Except," retorted Rolf, "that when we run the hills, Dirk and I, it is always shoulder to shoulder."

As the run progressed, alternating frequently between treacherous uphill slopes strewn with loose gravel, and steep downward inclines laced with trees which they had to dodge at speed, Dirk seemed to shake off his lethargy and became more sure-footed, so that after what Shaun guessed must have been five miles or so of hard slog, both he and Rolf were pleased to find Dirk only a pace or two behind.

There came a flat stretch by a river bank, and it was here that Dirk drew level so that he and Rolf were running together. Shaun, the least fit of the three, followed as closely as he could in their wake.

Rolf flashed a grin at him, but Dirk made no acknowledgement of his friend, and Rolf shot a glance back to Shaun which said more than any statement could have.

With the first of the two fells now behind them,

they enjoyed a stretch of level running before the ground began to rise once more, and they found themselves dodging the jagged boulders strewn around the base of the next slope.

As the incline increased, so did Shaun's discomfort, and the effects of his twentieth century lifestyle began to tell on him. As the others powered their way up the slope, he began to fall back, his breathing laboured, and he gritted his teeth in an effort to hide the fact that he was having difficulties.

Before the ground got really steep, Rolf called a halt. His own steady breathing indicated that he was fresh enough to continue, as Dirk seemed to be, and Shaun suspected that the break had been for his sake; though if it was, it wasn't made obvious.

They refreshed themselves from the stream that ran down the fell, and sat, their backs against a huge boulder, breathing deeply from the sweet, incredibly clear air.

Dirk seemed more at ease with himself now, but remained quiet, almost sullen, and didn't attempt to make conversation, only answering "yes" or "no" to any of Rolf's or Shaun's questions. Eventually, he rose and went over to the stream for another drink.

"Something troubles him more than the sadness in his family," confided Rolf. "I know it, but why he doesn't tell me..."

"I think it might be that he resents me," replied Shaun.

Rolf frowned at the new word for which the translating device in Shaun's ear had obviously been unable to provide an equivalent.

"Resent?"

"Yes, you know, not like us being friends."

"Why would he do that?"

"It happens sometimes," said Shaun. "Don't forget, you two have been friends for years. How would you feel if a stranger came along and took all the attention?"

"But you are my family."

"Yes, I am what Dirk would love to be – related to you. He loves you like a brother – I almost *am* your brother, but I'm a stranger as far as Dirk's concerned, an intruder, taking your friendship from him."

"No." Rolf shook his head. "I am sure you are wrong, I know Dirk too well." He looked over to where Dirk stood. "Right now, it is *he* who seems like a stranger. . ."

Their conversation was cut short by an awesome roar to their right which reverberated from the surrounding rock, a roar so chilling that for a moment Shaun's blood froze.

Hurtling from the bush came a giant of a bear, lips drawn back in a savage snarl, its claws raking dust as it advanced with a speed Shaun hardly thought credible. From the start it was obvious that it had targeted Dirk; it was equally obvious that Dirk didn't stand the faintest chance of getting out of its way in time.

Rolf moved with lightning speed, snatching a rock and throwing it in almost one movement.

It hit the bear high on the shoulder at the same moment as it lunged for Dirk's throat.

The surprise momentarily distracted it, and in the split-second that it took to regain its concentration, its momentum took it past its victim.

All it could do was lash out with one massive paw, and Shaun and Rolf watched in horror as the razor claws raked across Dirk's chest and the force of the blow sent him spinning into the shrubbery.

Rolf's knife was out and already in action as he cut a thick branch from a nearby tree, swinging on it, finally, to snap it at the cut.

The bear, meanwhile, having lost sight of its intended victim, turned, and fixing its tiny eyes on the other two, raced to the attack, its great shoulder muscles juddering with the effort.

Shaun, his heart pounding, had leapt to his feet, but sheer fright had, until now, rooted him to the spot; however, the sight of the charging, snarling beast was like an electric shock to his system, and he scrambled desperately to get out of the way.

He and Rolf actually went in opposite directions, and the bear, unable to decide which of them to choose, slithered and scrabbled from one possibility to the other for the vital seconds that it took them to get clear.

Rolf went sideways and upwards, straddling the huge boulder against which they had been sitting, the branch he had cut held firmly in his grasp.

Shaun ran across to the stream, the furthest distance he could put between himself and the bear whilst still having it in sight.

Instinctively, he felt that the moment he ran into the trees the animal would catch and tear him to pieces; so long as he could see it, there was a chance he might be able to dodge it – but not for long.

It swung to face him, saliva dripping from its jaws. Above it, Rolf was hacking furiously at the end of his branch, and already a long, wicked point was forming. Shaun cast around wildly for something with which to defend himself, and picked up a thin branch full of foliage, the only object in reach, and pitifully inadequate for the purpose, as he found when the beast, with another spine-tingling roar, charged him.

"Keep from him, Shaun!" Rolf shouted. "Weave and turn! Give me time!"

Shaun thrust the branch desperately into the crazed animal's face, and sidestepped.

How *much* time?

How do you convince a bear he shouldn't eat you until *you're* ready?

Twice Shaun managed to dodge the bear as it lunged at him, confusing it by parrying with the leafy branch, rather like a swordfighter would, and jumping aside to let it pass him as a bullfighter might do.

But now, his luck had run out. The branch lay broken and in tatters, the bear had learned quickly, and was not about to make the same mistake a third time.

A cold sweat broke out on Shaun's brow as the creature reared up on its hind legs and advanced on him, its huge bulk blotting out the sky as it did so. Somewhere in his terror-stricken brain, the notion that he was about to die was nudged aside momentarily by the memory of the escape disc which lay inside his pouch. If he used it, it would probably mean the end of his mission, but if he didn't, it would certainly be the end of his life.

Backing away, and with the bear not three strides from him, he fumbled in the pouch; his fingers touched the disc, but only succeeded in chasing it round the inside, failing to get a grip on it.

He fell backwards, and covered his face with his arm.

With a thud, a pair of feet landed by him, and almost at the same instant, came a roar of rage mixed with pain from the bear.

Looking up, Shaun saw that Rolf had leapt from the boulder he had been standing on, and had jabbed his pointed stake into the bear's leg. Immediately, the bear turned its attention to its attacker, leaving Shaun to roll free and witness what happened next.

Rolf backed away, matching the bear's advance step for step, his weapon, to Shaun's surprise, held loosely by his side, the point trailing on the ground by his feet. Another five paces, and he would be backed up against the giant boulder, his escape cut off. Then abruptly, Rolf changed direction; he ran three steps to his right, jammed the blunt end of his branch against a low protruding rock, and knelt on one knee, facing the bear, the sharpened end of the weapon cradled low, by his ankle.

The bear put in a burst of speed as he saw Rolf drop, assuming that its victim had fallen, and, reaching him, threw the whole weight of its body into the final assault.

Unbelievably, Rolf waited as the giant fell upon him, then, at the last split-second, brought the vicious point of the stake sharply up, rolling sideways as he did so.

His timing was perfect.

The stake pierced the bear's chest in the region of the solar plexus, driving itself through the heart, and protruding a good half metre between its shoulder blades. The roar was cut short as though a door had been slammed, and the creature was dead even before it hit the ground.

Such was the size of the animal, that probably nothing short of a strike such as that would have killed it; certainly no ordinary thrust could have done so much damage. Shaun was filled with admiration at the way that Rolf had used the bear's own weight to bring about its downfall.

Shaun released a breath he didn't know he'd been holding, his legs jelly.

"You did well, Shaun," said Rolf from where he was bent double, regaining his breath. "You gave me the time I needed."

Shaun blew out his cheeks. "*I* did well?"

Rolf straightened suddenly. "Dirk!" he cried, looking past Shaun. Turning, Shaun saw Dirk step from the bushes he'd been thrown into.

He walked across to them, calmly, unhurriedly, and with remarkable composure for someone who had, seemingly, suffered a bad injury.

He looked Rolf in the eye and nodded slowly. "You did well, Rolf," he said.

Rolf and Shaun gazed at Dirk's chest, then turned and exchanged looks of sheer amazement. His tunic was slashed where the bear's claws had ripped into him. Rolf reached, and held open the torn fabric.

Apart from four faint, pink lines across his ribcage, there was no evidence that Dirk had suffered the bone-crushing blow that they had both thought they had seen him receive.

A blow from which Dirk should have been crippled and in agony.

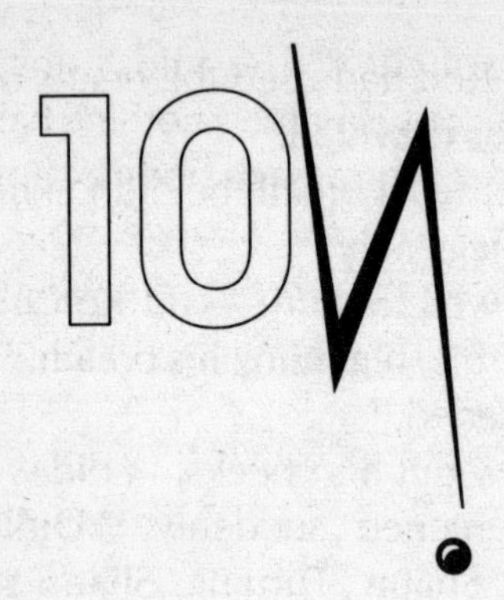

Vikings

"I have seen enough strange things in this day to last my lifetime," Rolf muttered to Shaun as they climbed.

"The bear can't have hit him as hard as we thought it did, that's the only real explanation," Shaun replied.

"Real?" returned Rolf. "I am no longer sure what is real and what is not."

So steep was the incline up which they now struggled, that running, even walking, was futile, and they were forced to haul themselves upwards.

Dirk was in front by maybe ten metres, with all his old agility back now, and not a trace of evidence that the encounter with the bear had affected him.

Rolf stopped and swept the hair from his eyes.

"This Phial I carry," he said, bringing it out and turning it over in his hand, "nothing has seemed right since I found it. My father's body disappears from the battlefield; we see the strange object which flies without wings; you come from nowhere – say you are my descendant; my friend Dirk becomes a stranger to me..."

"Look," broke in Shaun, "I don't know all the answers either, but we can't give up now..."

"In finding my father I will never give up," said Rolf, "but I am thinking maybe you should take this now and go, as you said you would, maybe then everything will be as it was, as it should be..."

Shaun hesitated. Should he do it?

Maybe his continued presence wasn't meant to be?

Maybe he was just making things worse by staying?

Who knew what had been affected by this intrusion into time?

Dirk's strangeness, even Oswold's disappearance might be connected in some way.

"...or maybe I should just destroy it now!" said Rolf, and his grip tightened around the metal tube.

"No!" cried Shaun.

Dirk, ahead, stopped and turned as he heard the cry.

Rolf thrust the Phial at Shaun. "Here," he cried, "take it! Take it! I grow weary with the madness of things!"

The fear showed in his eyes; not fear for his own

safety, but fear of the unknown; a fear that what he had witnessed so far might engulf him.

They held each other's gaze, and Shaun tried to keep an even voice. "Rolf," he said. "It wasn't until I realized who Oswold was that I realized the importance of freeing him."

"He is my father, who else would he be?"

"*Our* father," replied Shaun, "you said so."

Rolf lowered his arm, the Phial hanging by his side.

"Oswold was..." Shaun corrected himself, "*is* ... *will be* a very important figure in the fight for the country. I don't know ... I can't be sure ... if my arrival here has changed the way things are going to be, the way things *should* be. I have to stay to make sure ... I have to know that my being here hasn't interrupted anything. Can you understand this?"

Rolf took a deep breath, and let it out, and glanced up the hill to where Dirk stood motionless, watching silently, his bulk outlined against the sky.

"To say I understand would be to lie," he said, wearily, "but I see that you believe in what you say." He waved the Phial. "If this is your passage home, and yet you don't take it, you must have reason not to. And something tells me you want to be home as much as I."

"Believe me," said Shaun, "I do."

With a sigh, Rolf tucked the Phial back in his pouch, and nodded.

The climb became ever steeper, and Dirk dropped

back, placing himself alongside Rolf as they hauled themselves upwards, scrambling for footholds on the treacherous slope.

It was as they neared the summit that a rock crumbled beneath Shaun's inexperienced foot.

Shaun, at this point slightly ahead of the other two, slid, and his foot caught Rolf on the ankle. He gave a gasp of horror as he saw Rolf thrown sideways and disappear from view. Quickly, he scrambled to the edge and looked down, expecting the worst, to see that Rolf had just managed to grip a narrow ledge where he now hung, swinging, with a drop below him of some fifteen metres on to jagged rock. Dirk was also on the edge of the drop at the very point at which Rolf had fallen, and within reach of him. He could not have failed to appreciate the danger that his friend was in, but he made no move to go to his aid.

Shaun blinked in disbelief.

"Dirk!" he screamed. "Grab him! What are you waiting for?" And he threw himself across Dirk's muscular legs to act as a counter-balance.

Startled at the contact, Dirk looked round at Shaun.

"Grab him!" screamed Shaun again.

Rolf's fingers were white with the pressure of his flimsy grip, his feet scrabbling to find some niche which would serve to take weight from his hands; he had only seconds before his fingers would go numb and he would plummet.

For what seemed an age, Dirk stared into Shaun's

face. Then turning, he reached, took Rolf's wrist, and heaved him, almost effortlessly, to safety.

Rolf was shaken and grazed, but otherwise unhurt. He slapped Dirk thankfully on the shoulder, unaware of the hesitation that could have cost him his life. It was then that Dirk did something that neither of the others had seem him do since they had set out on the journey – he smiled.

Shaun himself had never felt less like smiling. What if Rolf had fallen? – and died? Where would that have left him? Rolf's death, so young, before he had had the chance to have children of his own, could only mean one thing – Shaun would never have been born!

And it was Shaun who had caused him to slip! His determination to carry through this particular bit of history that he had been thrown into grew stronger. Now he knew he *had* to make sure that the changes brought about by his intrusion into time had no adverse effects. Until Rolf was through this crisis and back on an even keel again, he had to stay, if only to compensate for the effects of his being here.

Ten minutes later, the three of them lay on the flat, grassy top of the fell, and gazed out across the bay they had struggled so hard to reach.

Below them, the sea lapped on to a long crescent of white sand, and there, resting in the shallows like great dragons, their prows pulled up on to the beach, lay a dozen Viking longboats. Great, sturdy craft, capable of dealing with the rigours of the sea over long distances, they accounted greatly for the success of the Danes, the Swedes and the Norwegians of this era, for no other nations of the time were building boats like these.

Spread out across the higher beach was the spectacle of the Viking encampment. It was an impressive sight. Shaun was able to identify the various tent structures. There was a large, bell-shaped tent central to the camp which he knew would house all the weaponry used on raids – shields, lances, swords, and such – and to its right, a smaller though similar one which he guessed was where the leaders would plan the stages of their campaign.

Towards the sea, stretched in rows from one side of the bay to the other, spaced neatly apart, were the smaller, peaked tents in which the warriors slept. Two other tented structures made up the camp, both in close proximity to each other, and both set back towards the rock wall which formed the enclosure of the bay.

The first was obviously a place to cook in, judging by the steam coming from its openings, and the utensils piled outside it; the other was a more grand-looking affair with nordic emblems painted on its surface. This was undoubtedly the commander's quarters.

There were plenty of men to be seen, sitting in

groups or walking about the camp, going about their duties, but it was a while before Rolf spotted the young girl leaving the cook tent.

She was Saxon, blonde, and wearing a robe, and as they watched, she walked to the far side of the beach to where a crescent of tall, pointed stakes had been driven into the sand and bound together with rope to form a semi-circle against the rock wall.

"A stockade!" hissed Shaun.

"Stockade?" echoed Dirk.

"A compound – that's where they're likely to keep any prisoners."

As he spoke, a gate was opened in the stockade and two guards allowed the Saxon girl to walk through before closing and barring it behind her.

From where they lay, it was impossible to see over the stockade wall, but Rolf's excitement at its discovery was clear to see.

A number of other prisoners could be seen now, mainly doing menial tasks such as carrying water, or stores, and Shaun could feel the anger boiling up in Rolf as he watched.

Rolf nodded grimly, but with some satisfaction. "I see two men who were in the battle yesterday," he said. "See how they are made to work like dogs."

"But at least we know that prisoners were taken yesterday," Shaun reminded him.

They worked out that the best way to get to the compound which held the prisoners would be to descend, to their left, to the sea, out of sight of the camp, then swim into the bay and, using the longboats as cover, swim to the far wall of the bay, from where, if it were dark enough, they could creep along the rock wall until they reached the stockade.

This agreed, they withdrew and began the descent, arriving at sea level in a matter of minutes. A jut of rock hid them from the bay, and it was this that they would have to swim around in order to get into the bay itself.

There was a swell on the sea, but thankfully no waves, which, Shaun imagined, could have easily smashed them to pieces on the jagged rocks. Rolf entered the water first, swimming smoothly and strongly with scarcely a ripple. Shaun followed, and Dirk slid after them, splashing noisily at first, then controlling his stroke, and lining up behind the other two as they bobbed like ducklings around the jut of rock and into the Viking bay.

The longboats looked bigger and even more menacing from this angle; sleek, powerful craft, wide-bodied to accommodate the warriors, but built also for speed when crewed over the water by the twenty pairs of oars which each one carried.

The first boat seemed to take them an age to reach, and until they made the safety of the stern, the possibility of them being spotted from the shore was very real indeed.

Once there, they crouched, feet just about touching the bottom, gathering their strength for the swim from stern to stern which would bring them to the other side of the bay and within at least striking distance of the stockade.

Rolf pulled his knife, a wicked grin on his face, and turning to the boat, carefully and deliberately prised out the rough, cast-iron nails at a joint in the planking just above water level.

"Let's see if they swim as well as they fight," he said.

Shaun nodded. Once filled with men, and in the open sea, the loose planking would prove a serious problem.

They swam underwater from boat to boat, taking it in turns to loosen a plank on each whilst the others swam on to the next one and did the same.

In this way they progressed as far as the eleventh of the twelve boats there, where they hit upon an unexpected problem.

Although it hadn't been obvious when they had first viewed the boats from the cliff top, probably due to the angle from which they had seen them, they saw now that there was a gap between boats eleven and twelve across which they could not swim without having to surface for air.

Peering around the boat, they could see a group of men half-way up the beach who appeared to be working on sail-mending, and some of them were facing the sea. It was going to be tricky.

Rolf took the lead, swimming underwater as far as he was able, before surfacing as gently as he could, eyes fixed on the group on the beach.

So far, so good; filling his lungs, he submerged and completed the crossing.

Shaun was prising the last nail from the planking on boat eleven as Dirk ducked below the surface and began to pull his way along to where Rolf was waiting. It was whilst he was underwater that a shout from the shore startled both Rolf and Shaun.

Had Dirk been seen?

Cautiously, they peered up the beach to see men on their feet, pointing in their direction and jabbering excitedly.

Had they seen the ripples on the water?

A sound out to sea caused Shaun to turn, and there, coming towards him, and not five hundred metres off, was another longboat full of Vikings!

And it was heading for the gap across which he had yet to swim, the gap across which Dirk was, at this very moment, underwater, swimming! If he was to surface now, there was no question but that he would be spotted.

Rolf and Shaun crept back around the stern of the respective boats they were by, tensed for the moment when Dirk's head would appear and the cry would go up.

A second later, and Dirk's head bobbed up

alongside Rolf. He had swum, unbelievably, the whole distance on one breath.

The two of them waded immediately into the shallows between the end boat and the rock wall, leaving Shaun, still unaware of Dirk's safe arrival, to disappear in a similar fashion.

Shaun retreated underwater to the far side of the next boat, the tenth, anxious to be well out of sight of both the occupants of the approaching boat, and the men on shore.

It was obvious that the warriors on the returning vessel had been involved in a battle, and as the prow of the boat ground noisily on to the shingle, men came running to assist those who could not assist themselves. The others, bloodstained and battered, lined up to file slowly from the deck. Shaun tucked himself close in alongside the boat he was hiding by, submerged up to his eyes, watching, as the boat's occupants filed past along the water's edge and on up the beach. Many bore wounds, and they all had the weariness about them that only prolonged conflict brings.

He saw that there were three Saxon captives who were shoved roughly ahead of the men holding them, their hands chained, but bearing their wounds and their captivity proudly.

The crowd thinned as the boat emptied, the babble of voices lessening as the exodus slowed to a trickle, and eventually, when the only sound was the steady slush, slush, of the waves on the shore, Shaun estimated that there was no one left on board. He glided to the stern, and leaned out cautiously to see if this was so. Unable to see as much as he needed to, he gripped the edge of his boat, put a foot against it, and leaned further.

He didn't account for the weeds on the boat's hull, and with a suddenness that brought an involuntary cry from him, his foot skidded on the slippery planking, caught the rudder, and propelled him clear of the boat. For a moment he thought he'd got away with it – no one on the shore seemed to be running in his direction. Then he looked up – and directly into the face of a lone Viking warrior kneeling in the stern of the newly-arrived vessel.

The expression on the man's face showed that he was hardly able to believe his eyes, but nevertheless, his reactions were swift enough.

Grabbing a nearby spear, he brought it up and braced himself for a throw, calling over his shoulder as he did so. There was an answering call from the beach, and the man shouted again, the urgency clear in his voice.

Shaun was powerless.

Unless he moved very quickly he was probably going to die, certainly he would be captured, there was nothing more sure, and his capture would prompt a search in which the others would surely be found. The crunch of gravel under running feet was followed by a hollow thud as those feet hit the deck above him and someone ran to the man's assistance.

Shaun had dipped swiftly into his pouch; the disc, buoyant in the water, leapt into the palm of his hand. The soldier above him drew back his throwing arm, hate twisting his features, obviously thankful for the chance to revenge the good men he'd seen today killed by the Saxon savages.

As his fist closed around the disc, Shaun, with no other option open to him, willed himself with all his strength to be back in his own year.

His head began to whirl, his vision swam, then, from the corner of his eye, he saw Rolf rounding the far boat, swimming to his aid.

Instinctively, he put his hand up, tried to wave his friend away, trying to hold on to his fast-fading consciousness long enough to be able to deter Rolf from what he was attempting.

He felt a physical jolt, and realized with a twinge of fear that he had done exactly what Jarrod had warned him not to do – he had failed to commit himself fully.

As in a dream, he heard Jarrod's words again, echoing somewhere in the back of his head: "...like an arrow to the target ... a good marksman needs commitment ... concentration..."

The Viking never got to throw his spear.

One moment the youth was there, floundering in the water, a perfect target, the next he was gone – vanished. The warrior who had run to the man's shout found a bewildered, tired soldier, gazing blankly at an empty sea. He put an arm around his shoulder and led him from the boat.

It had been a long, hard day.

Another couple of strokes, and Rolf would have been seen by either or both of the men as he swam to Shaun's rescue. As it was, the shock of seeing Shaun disappear before his very eyes stopped him dead in the water, and almost certainly saved his life.

As the baffled soldier allowed himself to be led away, so Rolf turned and swam silently back to where Dirk was waiting in the shallows between the last boat and the rock wall.

"Where is Shaun?" asked Dirk.

"Gone," said Rolf, "disappeared . . . vanished."

"Vanished?"

"Like that," said Rolf, and snapped his fingers.

Dirk's eyes narrowed at the sound. He looked at his own fingers, then clumsily tried to copy what he'd seen Rolf do.

Rolf said nothing, just sat with his back against the ship – and watched him.

Rual

Jarrod lay back on the rejuvenator couch in his rest room. Shaun's progress, he knew, was being overseen by his first officer, who was under strict instructions to contact him the second any change took place. For a long while now, it had been obvious that Shaun was accompanying the holder of the Phial on some kind of journey, and there was no way of knowing why that journey was being undertaken, when it might end, or when Shaun might decide to take over the Phial and return.

Jarrod's frustrations were tempered somewhat by the gut feeling he had that Shaun's delay was, for some reason, necessary, and probably due to an unforeseen circumstance. But his crew in the control room, lacking the instincts that Jarrod had inherited, and overtly encouraged by the calculated reactions of Silak Tulkan, were becoming sullen and suspicious. They would never actually voice their feelings, but he could sense that they were blaming him – obliquely blaming his unconventional methods – for the way things were going. Tulkan had made it clear by insinuation that he despised Jarrod's humanistic approach. To him, Shaun was merely a means to an end, a vehicle, a carrier, a way to get what was needed.

With such intransigence hanging in the air, it had seemed to Jarrod a good time to snatch a little rest time whilst he could. His body was resting, being soothed and relaxed by the impulses from the couch, but his keen mind was as alert as ever, going over and over the events which the sensors monitoring Shaun's metabolism had told him had taken place. The fatigue factor had indicated that Shaun had been pushing his body to the limits for some reason, and then, shortly before Jarrod had come to the rest room, the indicators showed that he had entered water and was swimming.

Jarrod was intrigued to know why Shaun was behaving the way he was, but what worried him far more was the knowledge that the Omnian agent was at large somewhere in the Year of the Phial, and that there wasn't any way in which they could warn Shaun to be on his guard.

His anger rose, causing the impulses from the

couch to react to compensate. He thought back to the time when Omnian treachery had touched his own existence, a time he would never forget, the most tragic day of his life.

His son, Rual, had been seven – had he been alive today, he would have been Shaun's age – and Jarrod well remembered the happiness he had felt as they both strolled through the Cephon woods near their home. Rual had been an active little boy, inquisitive too, and though Jarrod had warned him not to stray too far away, his enthusiasm had caused him to dash ahead of his father on the path they were taking. From beyond the trees, Jarrod heard him shout excitedly as he spotted some small animal.

Rual's voice came back to him now as he re-lived the moment:

"Father! Come and look!"

They were the last words he had ever spoken. The laser flash had lit the sky, throwing the trees briefly into silhouette, and Jarrod had frozen, horrified, before racing to the spot where he believed Rual to be.

"Rual! Ruallll!"

The Omnian laser wire had done its worst. Stretched wickedly across the path, Rual had had no chance of seeing it, no chance of survival, as the beam, broken by his passing, had shot to the nerve centre of his brain, killing him instantly. Jarrod had carried the limp body home, his hatred, that emotion that so many of his fellow Gravatites were unable to feel, simmering under his grief.

Everyone had been so sympathetic, had said how sorry they were, but there hadn't been one who had been able to understand his anger. Gravatites were not *meant* to feel anger; that sort of reaction lowered them to the level of the murdering Omnians. But Jarrod had found that his anger and his hatred had helped him to cope with the death of his son, for while he could hate, he could survive the tragedy, instead of falling to pieces with the grief.

He didn't want a world of hate and anger, but he was convinced that the Old Values could have their uses amongst the people of Grava, could give them back some individualism, and could help to combat the abuse they had suffered at the hands of the Omnians for generations.

But alas, whilst the present government of Grava was in power, the passive, peaceful, insipid way of life would continue.

How he admired the Earthlings for their initiative, their bravery, their adventurous natures. In spite of the faults that accompanied the human spirit, the anger, the violence of which they were undoubtedly capable, in Shaun he saw a prime example of how he longed his own people to be ... how he had hoped Rual would turn out to be.

He had kept Rual's room exactly as it had been on the day of his death; somehow it helped him pretend that he wasn't dead, that the room was waiting for him to return to.

His communicator leaped into life.

"Commander Jarrod, there is a development; come quickly, please."

Jarrod was running almost before his feet hit the ground, scattering startled technicians as he raced along the corridor and into the control room. Tulkan was leaning, arms folded, against a console, his arrogance barely masking a bitterness that hooded his eyes.

A glance summed up the situation.

It was "Condition Return", Shaun was on his way back! A further immediate check then confirmed the worst, even before Tulkan spoke a word; the return had been initiated by Shaun himself – he did not have the Phial!

"Velocity?" rapped Jarrod.

"2,000 Miclacycles."

"Activated when?

"Ten Earth-seconds ago."

Jarrod grimaced. It was a non-committed return.

His Miclacycle level should have been twice that to have had enough power to bring him back. At 2,000 Miclacyles he should have been well into the journey.

"He's not going to make it in one leap. He'll be lucky to make it at all!"

"Lucky for whom?" snickered Tulkan. "Not us."

Jarrod's face grew dark as thunder, and the coward in Tulkan made him stiffen as he saw it.

"Get to that Impulsator, now!" he roared.

Tulkan slunk back to his position, blinking away his humiliation.

Even as Jarrod spoke, the rate of Shaun's travel began to slow, the digits on the velocity-recorder dropping steadily as his passage through time and space began to run out of steam.

"We may lose him."

Tulkan stood by the monitor, whilst Jarrod took control of the main console, his deep intellect focused on the retrieval instruments which he knew he had to interpret with absolute precision if he were to help Shaun survive the journey, a journey which he knew was likely to have several stopping points for him. Shaun was set to skim the waters of time like a flat stone, touching here, touching there, and Jarrod could only pray that he reached his own year before he ran out of momentum.

Hands poised over the buttons like some eminent pianist, he counted down, silently, as the numbers ticked away.

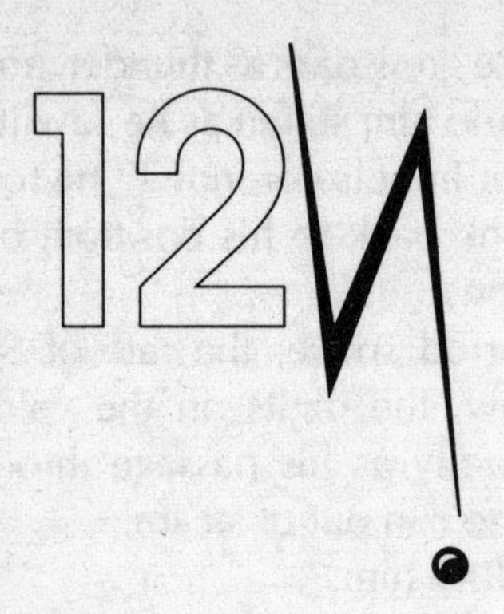

Lost

At first, the velocity with which Shaun had been thrown forward in time had pulled back the loose skin on his cheeks, but the G-force had lessened within seconds, and he now found himself tumbling incessantly, head over heels.

All around him was emptiness but for a blur of streaked light, with nothing on which he could focus even if he had been able to do so.

There was pressure on his ears, and a silence similar to being underwater, except for the thud! thud! of his own heart, like some distant drum. How long he tumbled like that, there was no way of knowing; it could have been a minute, it could have been an hour, but what did time matter under such conditions?

Gradually, he became aware that each somersault was taking longer to complete, his forward motion was slowing, and then, without realizing just when it had happened, he found he was no longer turning, simply drifting, face down, and the light was no longer streaking past him, but seemed to be frozen into an overall, all-enveloping glow.

He began to make out shapes below him, indistinct at first, then coming gradually more into focus. It was like trying to peer through several layers of plastic sheeting which were being removed one at a time. He saw green, flecked with white and black, which after a while took on the shape of a grassy hill with boulders and bushes; then suddenly he was falling, at an alarming rate, towards them.

As the grassy slope rushed at him, he braced himself for the impact, tucking in his head as his hands touched first, and rolling forward on to his feet. His momentum rolled him yet again before he lost balance, glanced with a crunch against a boulder, and came to rest, several revolutions later, against a shrub.

He eased himself into a sitting position, groaning with the pain which shot through his shoulder; his left leg, below the knee, was badly grazed and seeping blood. He saw that he was lying at the bottom of a hillock, and beyond and below him stretched a long, broad field dotted blue and red with wild poppies and cornflowers. There was a smell of something acrid in the air; it reminded him of Guy Fawkes Night, and he noticed several small puffs of white smoke at the far end of the field.

There was a distant noise, too, like the popping of balloons.

Still dazed by the fall, and unable yet to focus as well as he would have liked to, he sat for a while, gently testing the extent of his injuries and wondering just where it was he had ended up. He knew he had been thrown through time; he presumed he had been thrown *forward*, but how far?

Was he in his own year?

Somehow he doubted it, but there was nothing in sight which might give a clue as to which year he *was* in. And another, more worrying thought struck him: how would he move on if he had to?

Could he move on?

The disc! Maybe he could use it again? Feverishly, ignoring his painful shoulder, he scrabbled about in his pouch, only to realize with dismay that it was empty. Had he dropped it in the water of the bay, or had it been lost during the rough landing on the hillock?

He staggered to his feet. The distant popping sounds were more frantic now, and for a moment he thought it might be a sound within his head from some internal damage or other. He glanced to where the smoke still hung, and caught a bright flash like sunlight on metal.

There was something definitely happening in that direction, but what?

But he had more pressing problems on hand, and he dragged his befuddled mind back to the immediate task – the disc; if it was here he had to find it.

Step by painful step, he retraced the path he had taken, casting left and right, his task made more difficult by the profusion of red poppies, the same colour as the object he was looking for, scattered everywhere.

Half-way up the slope, the grass got longer and Shaun dropped to his hands and knees, sweeping the grass aside with his good arm, his hopes fading with every second.

He felt the vibration through his knees first of all, a sort of rapid drumming which, as it increased, he began to sense through his searching hand.

He knelt up, looked around; was he imagining it, or had the vibration actually become a sound?

Kneeling stock still, he listened.

The popping had stopped, the silence hung like a blanket, except that, faintly, the rhythmical drumming sound, rather like raindrops falling on a brolly, could be heard.

Another half a minute, and he was certain it was getting louder. He felt the ground again, though even through his knees he could feel that the vibrations were intensifying and were quite in time with the approaching noise.

Puzzled, he stood, and searched the distance.

He was higher than he had been before and, looking to where the smoke was drifting, he could see figures moving; figures in what looked like some kind of uniform, and the reflections of sunlight on bright steel fairly rippled amongst them.

Some kind of army, then?

The drumming sound had become a rapid thudding, and for the first time, he began to feel the ground actually shake beneath his feet.

With a suddenness which made him gasp, over the brow of the hill behind him, charged a line of horsemen. Without a break in their gallop, they careered headlong down the slope, to be followed immediately by a second line, then a third, and a fourth, until, within the space of five seconds, what had been a peaceful hilltop was covered with horses bearing men in blue uniform, sabres held high and gleaming, wild looks in the eyes of both horses and men, mouths wide in a barrage of screams, and the thunder of hooves became deafening.

As Shaun whirled to face them, and became transfixed with shock, the popping sound erupted again behind him, and he heard the whizz and spang of bullets, saw their effect as they cut trails through the grass around his feet, and broke splinters off the boulders.

Realization cut in – this was a cavalry charge, and he was right in its path!

He was powerless to do anything, even run, and as death bore down on him, not twenty paces away now, irrationally, his thoughts flew to his mother.

How would his death be explained to her? Or would he just become another "missing person", a young man who had set off for home and never got there?

With the leading horse almost on top of him, its wild eyes rolling, and the froth dripping from its mouth, he closed his own eyes in sheer despair, and he felt his knees buckle beneath him as blackness closed in.

He struggled to the surface of consciousness to find himself staring up at a blue sky. The thunder of hooves, still so vivid in his mind, drained away like a retreating clap of thunder, to be replaced by a sound so different as to be almost ludicrous – the twitter of birds.

The ache was still in his shoulder, the only tangible reminder of his fall on to the grassy hill, though the abject terror he had felt as the horse bore down on him still lingered like a spectre.

What was he doing here? Was he dead? Was this heaven?

He tried to turn, and found that heaven was the least likely place he could be. A thousand different points of pain shot through his limbs and his back. He could feel blood trickling down his cheek, and the more that clarity returned to his senses, the more he became aware of the needle-sharp pain which covered most of his body. Wincing with the effort, he managed to turn his head, and immediately realized the cause of his agony.

For some impossible reason, he was embedded in the centre of what seemed to be a thorn bush!

Each movement he made drove the thorns deeper into his flesh, already badly lacerated and bleeding from a hundred different wounds inflicted upon entry to the bush. The broken branches bore witness to the impact with which he had hit, presumably after being snatched away by the timeforce.

Thankful as he was that it had taken him from the path of the cavalry charge, he was unable to feel any elation for the position in which he now found himself, in fact the only feeling he had at this moment was profound agony, and all he could do was to try to remain as still as possible.

Peering through the branches of his living prison, he could see that the bush he was in formed part of a hedge around the garden of what looked like a mansion house and, as he looked, a man dressed in a long, grey coat with a broad collar, and with a tall, "stove-pipe" hat on his head, came from the house and began strolling around the garden, his hands behind his back.

Shaun's first impulse was to call to him, but he immediately thought better of it; apart from anything else, how could he begin to explain the situation? Yet he knew he would have to get help from somewhere, soon. Even to breathe deeply caused him pain, and he had to bite his lip to prevent himself from crying out.

He tried to concentrate his thoughts in an attempt to take his mind off what he was feeling, and watched as the man strolled over to the far side of the garden. He was sniffing the flowers, meandering; obviously he had time on his hands and seemed to be waiting for something, or someone.

He was a young man, probably in his twenties, though the severity of his dress made him look older, and Shaun thought he looked rather nervous.

Again Shaun juggled with the idea of calling out, but before he could do so, a girl in a maid's uniform came from the house with drinks on a tray which she placed on a table in the centre of the lawn before returning indoors.

Shaun eyed the drinks enviously; on top of everything else he had a raging thirst, and would gladly have given away his position at that moment for one sip of what he saw.

The blood from the cuts on his forehead was seeping into his eyes, and he was having to blink it away to focus, but what he saw next, despite his discomfort, caused him to blink with curiosity.

A young woman came from the house, causing the young man to become suddenly animated; obviously this was who he had been waiting for.

He strode quickly over to her, took her gloved hand and led her to the table where the drinks were, fussing around, and making sure she was comfortably seated before sitting himself.

What made Shaun stare, and momentarily ignore his discomfort, was the sight of her bright, copper-red hair, exactly the same shade as his own, and Rolf's; facially, she could have passed for his older sister.

Shaun didn't doubt for a moment that she was some distant relative, and wondered if, in these travels, he might be staying more or less in one place, and that only the years, and not him, were moving on. The cavalry had been on a hill; this mansion house, also, was on a hill.

Was it the same hill?

In the Year of the Phial, had it been one of the hills close by the Viking bay, and in his own time, would it be a hill close to his home town?

Would he ever get back to his own time? Was he due to be thrown forward again? He could only hope so, though the thought of being forced out of this bush, past those deadly thorns, made him shudder.

With a crack, the branches beneath him gave way, and he sank torturously into the bush, half turning as he did so, and he could not prevent a cry of agony as fresh thorns dug into him, and the old ones tore his skin. He found himself half-facing downwards, and gasped as he saw that the bush was overhanging the garden wall, with a drop of maybe thirty metres into a rock-strewn ravine below him.

The couple in the garden had heard his cry and had seen the bush shake, and now, puzzled, they had left the table, and were making their way slowly over to investigate. Shaun saw them coming from the corner of his eye as, with another lurch, the remaining branches parted, and with a strangled cry, he dropped completely clear of the thorn bush.

The belt around his waist caught around the crotch of a branch, and suddenly he was suspended, bleeding and frightened, over the massive drop. He heard the voices getting nearer, but a new peril drove the threat of discovery from his mind, as the belt rode up over his chest, one arm slipped through it, and suddenly it had tightened across his windpipe, strangling him.

His world spinning, he struggled to free his neck, just as a voice above him uttered, "What in the world . . .!"

He had been seen.

The next moment, the final branch that had kept him from falling split through, and Shaun, with half the thorn bush, went hurtling into space.

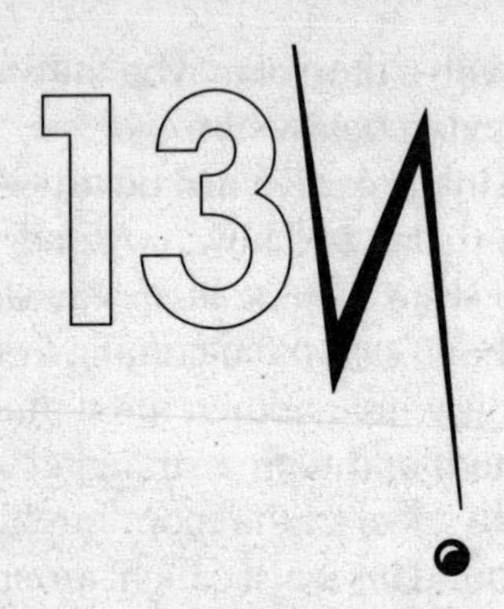

Found

Jarrod's long fingers drummed impatiently on the desk as his search-and-find facility, seeking Shaun, once again sifted painstakingly through time. The machine already had all the genetic data it needed; Jarrod had instructed Silak Tulkan to do that the minute that Shaun's abortive return had taken place, and upon Jarrod's instructions, the geneticist had lain down a search pattern of one hundred years between 1800 and 1900, a band of time into which, Jarrod had estimated, Shaun would fall judging by the registered strength of his initial commitment, and the surge level of the timeforce. There was no other way of finding him, other than by seek-and-find: comparing his chromosomatic make-up with every person in the land who had ever lived between those years. Even working at the speed of light, checking 186,000 body patterns each second, it took time.

The joy Jarrod had felt in finding Shaun after his first landing on the hillside had been short-lived; monitors had shown he was in a state of severe shock, and swift action had had to be taken to remove him from the life-threatening situation in which they had found him.

Tulkan hadn't liked it at all when Jarrod had impatiently knocked aside his hand and operated the touchpad that propelled the boy forward with a short burst of energy. Tulkan had since been trying to estimate how far that energy had taken him, and was making no secret of the fact that he didn't appreciate Jarrod's impulsiveness.

"As he is without the Phial, Commander Jarrod, I fail to see the urgency," he muttered.

Jarrod threw him a contemptuous look, and would have replied in kind, but suddenly the screen filled with information as the tracking device locked on to its find, and Shaun's new co-ordinates were thrown up. Tulkan's deft fingers keyed them swiftly into the computer, aware of Jarrod's rising anger.

Jarrod glanced at Shaun's metabolic indicator, and saw, with a pang of alarm, that he was now in an even more dangerous situation. His heart rate was at one hundred and thirty, his oxygen intake at a minimum, some form of strangulation seemed to be taking place, and death was imminent.

Again, with no time to programme destination co-ordinates, Jarrod slapped hard on the touchpad marked "Forward Projection".

He stared hard into Tulkan's eyes. "Set about fine-tuning the force of that thrust. I want that young man back."

The last thing that Shaun remembered seeing was the face of the girl with red hair as she peered into the thorn bush through which he had fallen, and he watched as she got smaller and smaller the further he fell. Racked with pain from his injuries, he hardly bothered to tense himself for the impact on the rocks in the ravine below, and it was a while before he realized that the impact was not about to happen. It dawned on him that he was no longer falling, but gliding at some speed through the same void of light that he had earlier experienced.

So weary was he that he felt he had been travelling all his life, that he was in a continuum from which there was no apparent escape.

Crushing despair descended upon him at the thought that he might spend forever just floating, touching Earth for brief moments, being bounced along like some rubber ball.

Shapes began to loom and vanish, loom and vanish, unclear shapes at first, then objects – some of which were recognizable, some not. A windmill; a ship with four tall funnels; a factory; a battletank –

items with no apparent connection, thrown together into one enormous scrap heap that was his mind.

Time, from being Shaun's first consideration, now became meaningless as he whirled around in that soup bowl of confusion.

Then, gradually, the grey of his surroundings began to be tinged with a purple hue which intensified slowly before becoming a blue, which in turn melted to green, then more rapidly to yellow, on to orange, followed by red.

The red held, and with it his whirling senses, and suddenly he was steady, his knees under his chin and hands clasping his ankles.

He became aware of a voice, distant, but growing louder, and which he recognized, eventually, as belonging to Jarrod. Opening his eyes brought a wave of sickness, as the room that he found himself in – the same cornerless chamber from which he had started his journey – shunted past his vision, only becoming stationary when he concentrated on the static lights around the top of the room.

Jarrod stared in horror at the image of the boy on his screen.

Not one area of his body was uninjured; some of the lacerations were deep and showing infection, whilst the monitors showed that he had a dislocated shoulder and a cracked tibula.

With haste, he beamed healing lasers into the chamber, sterilizing the wounds and promoting the skin tissue to rapid-heal. At the same time, he caused cellular nutrients to be discharged, boosting Shaun's sugar and protein levels, so that within seconds of arrival he was beginning to feel the benefits.

All the time, Jarrod talked to him, reassuring him, letting him know he was safe at last. Shaun's senses cleared remarkably swiftly as his body reacted positively to the treatment, and Jarrod, impressed by his powers of recovery, estimated that maybe ten Earth minutes in the chamber would improve his condition enormously.

Eventually, Shaun found the will to speak: "How long have I been away?" he croaked. "It seems like years."

"Just seven minutes," came the reply.

Seven minutes! The thought was so impossible he could hardly take it in. It *really* had seemed like a lifetime to him ... and for what? To what end?

"I let you down, didn't I, Jarrod? You and all your people."

Tulkan snorted, sceptically.

"You tried," replied Jarrod. "We can only thank you for that."

"Rolf needed my help."

"Rolf?"

"He has the Phial. I could have got it from him, I did have the chance, but I had to be sure I hadn't disturbed things ... certain events ... have to happen

... still have to ... I had to stay on ... do you understand?"

There was a pause, then Tulkan's voice, sullen: "Does Rolf still have the Phial?"

"I suppose so."

"You saw no one else?"

"Only Dirk – Rolf's friend."

"No one tried to take the Phial from Rolf?" asked Jarrod.

"Who would want to, but me?"

"The Omnians."

Shaun listened as Jarrod outlined the development that had taken place in the short time he had been away.

"The Omnians are clever creatures," Jarrod explained. "They are impostors, and can change their physical appearance to look like whoever they wish. It would be very difficult to know who this Omnian was or pretended to be."

A dreadful thought wormed its way into Shaun's mind.

"One minute more," said Jarrod, "and we can open the chamber." He turned to make final adjustments to the atmosphere.

"Jarrod?" Shaun's voice was tense.

"Yes?"

"Would the Omnian *act* like the person they impersonated?"

"Not necessarily so, but they do learn quickly, by imitation."

Shaun went white.

Jarrod showed concern as the instruments monitoring Shaun recorded the change in his mood. "Shaun, what is it?"

Shaun swallowed hard before replying. "Dirk!"

"You mean..."

"Dirk is the Omnian! I know it! Can you send me back again?"

Jarrod could hardly believe his ears.

"Jarrod? Did you hear what I said?"

"Why ... yes, of course, but..."

"Then do it ... please!"

"Send him!" snapped Tulkan.

"Shaun..." began Jarrod.

"Quickly! Rolf's in danger! If he dies, *I* die! More than that, if he doesn't rescue his father, the whole of my civilization will be affected!"

Jarrod's brain raced. Could he justify sending Shaun back after all he'd been through?

"Jarrod, I have to finish off what I started, don't you see that? I can't just leave it now, not knowing what I know!"

Still Jarrod paused.

"I'm setting the co-ordinates now!" said Tulkan.

"Send only on my orders!" Jarrod shouted and Tulkan reluctantly stood back. "Shaun," he continued more softly. "Take care."

"I will," said Shaun, "and Jarrod – you'll have your Phial . . . if it's at all possible."

Shaun's injuries were well on the way to recovery as the pad was pressed which sent him unerringly back. The whistle of the projection mechanism had barely died when the adjutant stepped up to Jarrod's position.

"Sir," he said.

Jarrod continued to stare vacantly at the pod, a thousand thoughts swimming in his mind. There was little doubt that the chances of retrieving the Phial were much less than they had been, and now there was the added complication of the business that Shaun now seemed involved with – whatever that was.

"Sir," the adjutant repeated.

There had always been a risk that Shaun's appearance in the Year of the Phial would alter some aspect of history, but Tulkan had always insisted that the risk was so small it was negligible.

Jarrod swung to face Tulkan, and checked in surprise as he saw the reason why the adjutant had been trying to gain his attention. "Drago," he exclaimed, "what are you doing here?"

His friend the councillor stepped forward from the doorway by which he had just entered; the seriousness of his usually cheerful countenance gave a hint as to the nature of his visit.

Whilst the two crew members of the ship that had

brought him from Grava left to debrief and to rest, Drago took Jarrod's arm and steered him to the quiet of the sub-space communications module behind the partition screening.

"We must talk," he said.

Once seated, Drago lost no time in coming directly to the point; they knew each other well enough to know that each preferred straight-speaking.

"One Grava hour ago, the Sporon disease claimed the life of the governor."

Jarrod shuffled uneasily; the news was bad, but he had a feeling that was not all that Drago had come to tell him. News of the governor's death could have been relayed to him on the holocube.

Drago continued. "The Higher Council have elected me to take his place."

Jarrod beamed. "That's wonderful," he said. "I can't think of anyone better."

"I can," said Drago. "You."

"Me?"

"If you so wish it."

"But . . . but it's *you* they want – you just said so. Didn't you accept?"

"In part. I told them I had to speak to you first."

"I don't understand. . ."

Drago looked him full in the eye. "Don't you?" he said. "Aren't we both Cry-borns? Haven't we always shared the same ideals, the same hopes, harboured the same dreams for Grava, since we were boys?

Haven't we always wanted what was best for our planet, for its people? Don't we both agree that the way ahead lies not with the suffocating passiveness that we all suffer from? Don't you want to see Grava stand up for itself against the Omnians?"

"Well, of course ... you know I do ... but..."

"Then join with me, Jarrod. What I'm proposing is a joint governorship, you and I. Together we can make the planet what it used to be."

Jarrod was stunned. The possibilities crowded on top of his doubts. Wasn't this the chance he'd dreamed of – to be able to re-introduce Old Values into his society, the chance to inject into his people the desire for life and all that it could offer? To re-educate them them towards being a better, more wholesome, more *feeling* people?

He turned to Drago. "You think we could?" he asked.

"I *know* we could," replied Drago, "and so do you."

Jarrod deliberated, then nodded. "I think we could."

Contact

As the sun began to dip to the horizon, Rolf, shivering now as he crouched in the shallows, looked across to where Dirk sat, the water lapping to his muscular waist.

The loss of Shaun, so sudden and so mysterious, had shocked Rolf to the core, and had made him realize just how vulnerable his own position was – particularly with regard to Dirk.

He was aware that, since the two of them had been alone, Dirk had not taken his eyes off him for a moment.

Furthermore, almost every move that Rolf had made, whether it was to stretch his cramped limbs, or to peer around the boat by which they crouched, Dirk had, for some reason, copied. Rolf had even made one or two unnecessary movements just as a check, and sure enough, Dirk had copied these too.

On top of this, he had been uncharacteristically talkative considering how silent he had been since the start of the journey, almost like the old Dirk, though, Rolf noted, not quite.

Dirk talked, in particular, about friendship; not just *their* friendship, but about people in general, and the way in which they could rely on each other for help, as Oswold could on Rolf, and as Rolf had begun to rely on Shaun.

Although he tried not to show it, Rolf found Dirk's sudden obsession with the idea of friendship worrying. The Dirk he knew wouldn't have had the need to talk the way he did.

Something had brought about a change in his friend which was as mysterious as any of the events that had taken place so far, and Rolf was beginning to think that he knew just why that change had taken place, though for the moment, he said nothing.

Peering up the beach, Rolf could just see the first few pointed stakes which made up the stockade wall; the rest were out of sight behind the tents.

Along the beach, he could see that men were beginning to light camp fires in readiness for the approaching night; a mouth-watering smell was drifting from the cook tent.

Dirk's voice hissed close to Rolf's ear: "We can make the stockade easily with care."

Rolf looked him in the eye. "I am going alone," he said.

Dirk's face took on a puzzled expression. "But we are friends," he said.

Rolf gripped his dagger handle, ready for any reaction to what he was about to say. For a long moment he studied the face he had grown to know so well over the years, then steeled himself, and spoke what was in his heart.

"Who are you?" he asked.

Alarm showed in Dirk's eyes. "I am Dirk."

Rolf shook his head. "You are not Dirk," he said. "You look like Dirk, but you are not he."

The impostor became agitated, his eyes took on the look of a hunted animal, and Rolf prepared himself for the fight he had half-anticipated.

Instead, the lookalike's shoulders sagged, like a sail without wind. "When did you know?" he asked.

"When we were on the cliff looking down on this camp. The girl we saw, the one who walked from the cook tent to the compound, that was Rona. Rona who was your sweetheart until she was taken two years since, yet you did not recognize her. And Edric was plain to see. Edric who taught us all we know about wrestling, who still wrestles with us each day, and has done since we were small. But you did not recognize him. Then I knew."

They stared silently at one another.

"Who are you?" repeated Rolf.

"One with a mission," came the reply.

"You seek the Phial," said Rolf. It was not a question, but he received a nod in reply.

"And my friend, Dirk, does he live?"

"He lives."

"Truly?"

"Truly, he lives."

"Had you said 'no', your own life would have ended here," growled Rolf.

"He lives and is unharmed."

Rolf relaxed just a little. "You have a name?" he asked.

"Kal."

A light seemed to have gone out in Kal's eyes, and Rolf no longer felt imminently threatened by his presence, but even so, he remained vigilant.

"You have done me no harm, Kal, and since you tell me that Dirk is alive, I have no quarrel with you. Until I die, I will wonder how you came to look so like my friend that I believed you to be him. . ."

Kal made to speak, but Rolf silenced him with a raised hand. "Tell me not! There are some things that no one was meant to know, and enough strangeness has taken place already." He stared, expressionless, at the stranger. "Go your way, I must go mine . . . and Shaun's Phial goes with me."

"I can help!" said Kal, a hint of desperation in his voice. "I am your friend!"

"Friendship springs from trust," said Rolf, and turned to crawl warily from the shallows.

"I have learned this!" hissed Kal.

"Then learn this, also," whispered Rolf. "A friend asks nothing in return for friendship – the Phial stays with me!"

Keeping close to the rock wall, and with his face turned to the fires, from where danger was most likely to come, Rolf inched his way over the soft sand, slithering snake-like across the first open stretch, and resting only when the first of the smaller tents was between him and the rest of the camp.

So close was he to these tents, pitched in rows from the wall to mid-beach, that if he had stretched out he could have touched them, and there was no way that he could know whether or not any of them were occupied. Glancing back, he saw Kal, kneeling still in the shallow water, watching his progress. Though the shape was that of Dirk, the expression on the face, now that no pretence was needed, showed that Dirk's personality was not inside the body; Kal looked, somehow, lost, sad, and if Rolf hadn't reminded himself of the way that Kal had deceived him, and Shaun, not to mention the real Dirk, he could have felt sympathy for him.

Instead, he turned and concentrated on the task in hand. At all costs, he had to reach the compound unseen, and there were a number of gaps between the rows of tents that he had yet to cross. Already he was working out a plan for contacting the prisoners inside and, as part of his plan, he snatched up a flat piece of driftwood and tucked it into his belt.

He had known since spotting Edric, the wrestler, that his father must be inside the prisoner's compound. Edric and Oswold had been in the same battle the day before; what was less certain was the condition that Oswold might be in. Edric had appeared to be unwounded, but Rolf could only hope that his father had not sustained serious injury – or, by now, worse. One by one, the rows of tents slipped by him, and he crossed each gap with renewed confidence.

He was about half-way to the compound now, crouched by the last tent in the line. Between that tent, and the pointed stakes of the stockade wall, there was nothing but bare, open sand. The cook tent was set back towards the middle of the beach, and through its cloth walls, Rolf could see the glow of the main camp fire beyond it, around which the shapes of men coming and going could be seen in silhouette.

The gate to the compound was, thankfully, around the far side of the stockade wall, though Rolf could see one of the two guards who stood by it. From time to time, this guard would turn and stroll along the wall in Rolf's general direction before turning to stroll back to his position.

Without the benefit of cover, Rolf suddenly realized, with a lurch of disappointment, he had very little chance of reaching the compound without being seen either by the guard or by someone at the fire who might casually glance his way. As he lay, wondering what course of action he might take, the flap of the cook tent opened, and a giant of a man wearing a greasy leather apron and carrying a large, wooden bowl emerged. The bowl appeared to be full of bones and offal, and the man called over to the guards, jokingly offering the contents to them, before trudging with it in the direction of the spot where Rolf was lying.

Rolf watched him with growing dismay as the man tramped nearer and nearer over the sand, cursing once or twice as the odd bone fell from the pile in the bowl.

It was then that Rolf saw the pit that had been dug against the rock wall not half a dozen strides ahead of him; from it came a faint smell of rotting meat. In a flash, it came to him that the cook was heading for the pit to deposit the contents of the bowl he was carrying, and in doing so, was bound to see him. A muffled cough close by to his right startled him, and he realized that the tent he was crouched by had at least one occupant; he couldn't even dodge round to the front of the tent as the cook walked past.

The man was a mere six paces away now, and Rolf coiled himself like a spring, his dagger drawn, determined to fight if he had to, but preferably to make a good escape in one direction or another, most probably up the rock wall, which, though not vertical, was still a steep climb.

If he were to be captured, then all hope of freeing his father would be lost for ever.

The guard on the stockade gate gave a shout, and the cook stopped and turned to him, a laugh bubbling in his throat, his huge shoulders shuddering with mirth. For seconds vital to Rolf, the two men exchanged good-humoured banter, and Rolf was able to scour the rock wall, his experienced eye taking in every crevice and lip, working out the quickest way that he could scale it.

Satisfied, he sheathed his dagger, and waited.

A thought struck him.

If he went now, instead of waiting to be discovered, he might gain a good six metres.

Taking a deep breath, he tensed his muscles, and was on the point of leaping up, when a voice sounded, at a low whisper, close behind him.

"For this, Rolf," breathed Kal, "I ask nothing in return."

Rolf spun round, annoyed that his concentration had been broken.

His annoyance changed to bewilderment, as Kal reached over, squeezed Rolf's shoulder in a grip of unmistakable affection, and before Rolf could even guess at his intentions, Kal was up and running like a deer towards the camp fire.

As a diversionary tactic, it could not have worked better.

He was seen before he'd taken four strides, and the shout went up, firstly from the guard, then from others attracted by the urgency in his voice.

The cook dropped the bowl and gave chase, as Kal fairly flew over the sand and around the cook tent. It would have been easy for him to have shot off at a tangent through a less occupied section of the camp, but instead, he headed straight for the fire around which scores of Vikings were gathered.

Rolf watched from hiding, ducking only when the soldier from the tent he was alongside dashed out to join the chase.

Kal weaved and ducked with almost supernatural speed, evading outstretched arms, eventually reaching the camp fire where he gave a jump which brought gasps of incredulity from all who witnessed it.

He cleared not only the fire, but the heads of those who stood around it, and the last that Rolf saw of him was as he was at the zenith of that graceful leap, lit from below by the firelight, his feet coming together to land on the other side.

Within moments, every soldier in the camp, with the exception of the two guarding the compound gate, had fled in the same direction, yelling, gesticulating, chasing the intruder until the night gloom swallowed them in their pursuit.

Rolf's pang of gratitude steeled his determination, and he ran swiftly over to the stockade wall, safe in the knowledge that the eyes of the guards were on other things, and dragging the piece of driftwood from his belt as he did so.

A hubbub of voices from inside the compound told that the prisoners were aware that something was going on. Rolf scratched his name into the wood with the point of his dagger and hurled it high over the top of the wall.

A dull thud, and a cry of surprise told their own tale as Rolf waited impatiently, his back pressed close to the wooden stakes, casting wary glances down the beach to where the distant cries of anger could still be heard.

There was a hush now on the other side of the wall, followed by a scrambling, and the next moment, a head appeared briefly above him, and Rolf heard another thud as the spyman dropped from the shoulders on which he had been standing.

In the stillness that followed, much whispering could be heard, and eventually, a voice, directed at him, drifted through a gap by Rolf's knee.

"Rolf, son of Oswold?"

Rolf dropped to one knee, saw an eye peering at him. "My father. He is here?"

"Aye."

"Let me speak with him, quickly."

"Aye."

That "aye" brought a flood of relief to Rolf; it was the proof he had been looking for that Oswold was alive.

The first eye disappeared, to be replaced by a succession of eyes belonging to men eager to see this Saxon youth who had penetrated the Viking camp so effectively.

The distant enemy voices had quietened now, leaving Rolf to speculate on what might have happened to Kal. It seemed likely that he would be caught; in the ordinary way of things, there seemed no way in which he might evade such a number of men for long, but then again, as Kal had proved, he was not ordinary.

After what seemed an age, a familiar eye pressed itself to the gap, and Rolf heard the rich, warm voice of his father call his name.

"Father!" breathed Rolf in relief.

"My son!" A pause, then... "You have done well!"

"There is much left to do," whispered Rolf. "How best to free you?"

"With a dagger we can cut the ropes binding this wall."

Without hesitation, Rolf slipped the hilt of his dagger through the slit, and watched as it was swiftly drawn out of sight.

"We are eighty-five," continued Oswold, "some too injured to fight, and we are weaponless."

"The villagers," said Rolf. "I can bring the villagers."

"Do that, and we will be waiting. When the time is right, we will join the attack."

"Without weapons?"

"A Saxon with bare hands is worth three Dane men with swords, but if we can but breach their weapon place, then they will have a true fight on their hands."

"I will leave *now*; with luck I will make the village by nightfall."

"Strength go with you, Rolf; take great care."

Inspired by his father's words, Rolf turned, checked once for the guards, and dashed back, like a hare, over the open stretch of sand to the shelter of the tent by the offal pit.

He had already reasoned that the surest way back to the village would be the way he had come with Shaun and Kal, using the cover of the longboats, and making the easy climb back up to the clifftops.

If only he didn't feel so tired.

Out on the beach, a lone, authoritative voice was shouting instructions, and a group was beginning to gather by the commander's tent. Rolf cautiously made his way back down the line of small tents towards the sea, anxious to be on his way, yet eager, at the same time, to know what success Kal might have had in evading his would-be captors.

By the time he got back to the shallows by the end longboat, it was clear that the Vikings, castigated by their commanders, were about to begin a thorough search. Groups were being despatched to various sections of the bay, and Rolf knew that, as a part of that search, the longboats would come in for particular scrutiny. He either had to find another way out of the bay, or hide until the search had been completed.

He looked around him. Already it was too late to make his way back up the beach to a point where he might climb the cliffs. His eye travelled back down the rock wall to where he was standing; as it neared the sea, the wall sloped sharply so that if he were to climb maybe three times his own height up from where he now was, he would find himself in the next bay. Perhaps he could lay in hiding there until the search had been called off?

In less time than it would take to tell, he had scaled the wall and dropped down on the other side.

It was not ideal.

There was a scarcity of boulders he might hide behind, and it occurred to him that since he had found the climb easy, so too might the searchers.

There were, however, two bushes which between them produced a fairly dense foliage, and whose branches just showed above the ridge separating the two bays.

More in hope than in certainty, he crawled in amongst the leaves, to find to his surprise that the cover they gave was more than adequate, and that, furthermore, it was comfortable.

Too comfortable.

The weariness of twenty-four action-packed hours on his feet crept up on him, and despite attempts not to, in under five minutes he had fallen fast asleep.

Capture

Shaun's projection back to the Year of the Phial was not as accurate as Jarrod would have liked, but that was all to the good, as it turned out.

A pin-point accurate return would have placed him chin-deep in the open water in which he had been floundering when the timeforce had dragged him away, and the group of Viking warriors sitting on the beach only metres away would have seen him instantly. Luckily, he materialized in the shallows close by the stern of the last boat, and heard the men even before he peered around the hull to see where the voices were coming from.

They were mending sails, and beside them lay a pile of boxes which, Shaun presumed, had been unloaded from one of the boats. As he watched, a couple of Saxon prisoners came and went, each taking one of the boxes up the beach to a store tent, only to return for others.

Shaun's first thoughts were for Rolf. Had Dirk, or whoever he was, killed him and got the Phial?

The fact that he'd just been transported suggested not, though, for all he knew, the chromosome alignment that made a transportation possible might not need *both* people to be alive.

Then a further, more alarming thought struck him. What were the chances of him (Shaun) returning to his own year without a disc *or* a Phial to help him?

The plain, chilling, answer was – none!

Had he sealed his own fate by insisting on a return? Had Jarrod assumed he still had the disc? Surely they had some way of retrieving him, and wherever the Phial was, they would have tracked it? He could only hope so, but hope was little comfort at a time like this. The doubts and uncertainties crowded upon him.

From the position of the sun, it appeared to be early morning – but which morning?

Had he missed one whole night . . . or two?

What if the difference in time between his own year and this one meant that he had arrived *earlier*? Was this the morning of the day that they had first entered the bay of the Vikings, and if he waited, would he actually see Rolf, Dirk, and *himself* come swimming along the boats from stern to stern?

He began to feel misplaced, disorientated and

unsure; he badly needed the security of knowing just where it was he fitted in.

The group of men were still on the beach, and whilst they remained there, it meant that he was forced to remain where he was, though even if the coast had been clear, there wasn't a single thing he could think of that he could usefully have done.

He desperately needed to contact Rolf; only then would things begin to make sense.

A "plop!" to his right startled him, followed by a second a bit nearer, and in the clear water Shaun saw two pebbles settling.

With a sigh of relief, he looked around, just as a third struck his shoulder, but try as he might, nowhere could he see Rolf – for there was no doubt in his mind that it was he.

The rock wall was bare, and its ridge was stark and empty against the blue sky, except for the top branches of a bush peeking over inquisitively.

A movement amongst the leaves of the bush caught his eye, and a splash of copper colour in the green told him what he wanted to know. Rolf, like himself, was in hiding, and trapped by the presence of the Viking sail-menders who looked like they might be set to continue their task for the rest of the day.

As the morning wore on, and the sun rose higher in the sky, Rolf began to suffer.

He had not eaten, or drunk, for a good thirty-six hours, apart from a few edible berries he had found on the bush he was now crouched in, and he knew he would have to find sustenance of some kind very soon, or become too weak to move.

He had been excited to find Shaun back in the shallow water, and now that he had made contact with him, it gave him a little more hope than he had had before. Since he had woken, he had been cursing himself for falling asleep and missing his chance to bring help from the village, and he knew that his father and the other prisoners in the compound would be awaiting the villagers' return by the minute.

Even if he was able to get away at once, this instant, it would be another day, at least, before he could rally the men and lead them back here. By then, the prisoners might have decided to break out on their own, now that they had his dagger; if they did, Rolf knew they would be slaughtered – and it would be all his fault.

A shout from the beach brought his head up sharply.

Peering between the branches, he saw that a man was beckoning the group on the beach.

A glance showed that Shaun had heard it too, and hope rose in Rolf's chest, competing with the gnawing hunger in his stomach, that the stalemate situation might soon be over. Sure enough, in response to the call, one by one, the men left their work and began to amble up the beach for what looked like a meal break.

Rolf wasted no time.

As the last man turned away, he left the anonymity of the bush, and slipped over the ridge – then froze against the rock as the man turned back, reached into a bag, and took out a container. Idly, he removed the stopper, lifted the container to his lips, and drank. Having finished, he let his eyes wander over the rocks as he replaced the stopper. Just at the point where he would have discovered a young Saxon clinging, lizard-like, to the rock face, a shout from his companion turned his head, and dropping the container into the bag, he joined his retreating colleagues.

Rolf took no further chances. Carefully slipping back over the ridge, he skirted the bush, and scrambled down to drop into the water below, from where he swam around the miniature headland into the Viking bay to join a delighted Shaun.

"Rolf – the Phial...?" hissed Shaun as Rolf approached.

Rolf nodded. "I have it," he whispered, and the next moment they were standing, chin-deep, next to each other. "It's good to see you again."

Shaun nodded. "You too."

"You came back for the Phial?"

"I came back to help."

Rolf shook a bewildered head. "What kind of

creatures live in your time, Shaun, that can change to look like another?" he asked.

"You mean Dirk?"

"He called himself Kal. I'm glad my time is here, now, where we know who is who."

"What happened to Dirk?"

"He told me that Dirk is alive and unharmed," said Rolf.

"Do you believe him?"

Rolf considered. "He made it possible for me to reach my father . . . put his life at risk to do so. Yes, I believe him. I think that, in the end, his intentions were better than when we first met him."

Shaun waited, expecting more, but Rolf gave a shrug. "Kal, I think, is another story, for another time," he said. "Now we must put all our efforts into reaching the village. I must bring help."

"Right," said Shaun. "Quickest way is to swim back the way we came. . ."

"No!" cut in Rolf. "That is the safest way, but not the quickest."

"Then what is the quickest?"

"Straight through the camp."

"What?"

"Follow me, I have a plan."

So saying, Rolf waded boldly from the water and approached the boxes he had seen the Saxon prisoners unloading.

"Rolf. . .?" hissed Shaun, but he had no option but

to follow him, though serious doubts about the sanity of the move loomed large in his mind. Indeed, Shaun could only guess at the extent of Rolf's suffering right now; had his condition, the hunger and thirst he must be feeling, affected his brain? Shaun knew he himself would be suffering in a similar way had it not been for the nutrients he had received in the transfer chamber, and if Rolf was acting recklessly through fatigue, it could mean disaster for both of them.

As soon as Rolf shouldered one of the boxes, Shaun saw the plan, but the possibilities of it working were not quite as clear.

If they could pose as prisoners they *might* be able to reach the far side of the beach, but what then? Rolf pointed with his chin, and following his gaze, Shaun saw, in the far corner of the bay, the chance of escape up a more gentle slope which seemed to lead over the hill and in the general direction that they had taken on approach to the bay – the direction in which Rolf's village lay.

He shouldered a box himself, and nodded to Rolf. Rolf, however, had one more thing to do. Kneeling, he reached into a bag, took the container of water he had seen the sail-mender drink from, and lifted it to his lips.

Even in his extreme need, he paused long enough to check whether Shaun wanted a drink, and seeing the shake of Shaun's head, he drained the container dry, a look of near agony on his face.

Careful to keep the boxes on their shoulders between them and the rest of the camp, they slowly threaded their way up through the tents, lowering their heads as they passed Vikings, homing in, in as straight a line as possible, on the far strip of hillside which ran down to the bay, and up which a bare, narrow path could faintly be made out.

Shaun went ahead of Rolf, passing the trestle tables outside the cook tent, laden with cooked meat, game, venison, pork, and continued on as far as the Command tent before turning, as casually as he could, to check that Rolf was with him.

Shaun's heart almost froze.

Rolf was standing by the meat-laden tables, the box still on his shoulder, cramming handfuls of meat from the plates into his mouth, casting around continually in case someone should come along. For what must have been a full thirty, breath-holding seconds, Shaun watched in dread, rooted to the spot with apprehension, as Rolf bolted food into his empty stomach, then turning, he wiped an arm across his mouth and grinned wickedly at his friend.

The grin slid from his face as the tent flap flew back, and the giant cook shambled out, almost falling over Rolf as he did so.

The mountainous Viking took one disbelieving look at the demolished pile of food, took in Rolf's greasy jaws, and exploded, rending the air with an almighty roar of anger. He roared again, this time in pain, as Rolf dropped the corner of the heavy box full on to his toe, and ran.

Shaun's first instinct was to do the same, but something told him not to. He was far enough distant from Rolf not to be associated with him, and when three burly warriors grabbed Rolf in mid-flight, Shaun knew he had done right to hold on to his box.

Whilst he had it, he was anonymous, nothing but a box-carrier, a bystander.

There was nothing he could do to help Rolf now: he was struggling like a captive animal, but his capture was a certainty. Yet, for all of this, their original plan was still intact, and Shaun realized, as he watched the drama before him unfold, that it was up to him to carry it through; up to him to reach the village and to bring help as fast as he was able. There was no one else who could.

Turning, he forced himself to make his way as slowly as ever, trying to ignore the commotion behind him, shutting his ears to Rolf's cries of anger, pain and frustration, as the edge of the camp and the start of the path up the hill drew nearer with every step.

Rolf, for his part, was determined not to be captured quite so easily. Apart from anything else, he had seen that Shaun was still on course for escape, and he was determined to do his utmost to create a diversion. The three men who held him soon knew they had a fight on their hands.

A well-aimed heel caught one of them in the lower stomach, bringing him to his knees with a gasp, whilst a vicious elbow in the face split the nose of the second man, stunning him with the pain.

It was fortunate that Rolf had been practising wrestling all his life; the third man suddenly wondered why the world had turned upside down, and why he was now gazing at the sky, gasping for breath, with all the wind knocked out of him.

At this stage, Rolf might easily have run, but the fight was on him now, a red mist of anger before his eyes, and knowing that capture was inevitable wherever he ran to, he determined to face them here sooner than somewhere else.

Consequently, he turned his defence into attack. With four men lying incapacitated around him, he ran headlong at a fifth who was rushing to the scene, catching him full in the chest with both feet, sending the man spinning away like a leaf in a wind.

He ducked beneath another's outstretched arms, then, stiffening his legs, heaved the man over his back, where he fell awkwardly against a table and lay motionless.

But more men were now on hand, and they moved in quickly to contain the rebellious Saxon.

Rolf managed to avoid two attempts to rush him, and to deliver a bone-crunching blow to the jaw of one of his attackers, but by the time he'd turned, the others were upon him, pinning him to the ground by sheer weight of numbers.

Shaun looked back as he reached the path which led up the hillside, in time to see Rolf's limp body carried roughly by four soldiers, each holding a limb, up to the stockade gate, which was opened just wide enough for him to be dumped inside.

It was impossible to tell how badly Rolf had been hurt. Shaun dismissed the thought that he might even have been killed; if that had been so, and his own ancestral chain had been broken, he would have been aware of it, of that he felt sure.

He tried to imagine what it would be like for the prisoners to see the one person they had pinned all hopes on, captured and enslaved like the rest of them, and particularly, what it would be like for Oswold to have the battered body of his son thrown at him in such a manner.

Shaun offered a prayer that Rolf wasn't too badly hurt, then quietly laid aside the box behind which he had been hidden, and sprinted determinedly up the hillside.

Encounter

Shaun estimated that with a little luck, he would reach Rolf's village by nightfall – providing that he could find his way there. A sense of direction had never been one of his strong points, but, one way or another, come darkness, he would have to have reached his goal; the thought of trying to find his way in the dark in this unfamiliar and hostile territory didn't appeal to him one bit. Once out of the bay and over the hill, he cast an eye at the position of the sun and lengthened his stride a little, the loose stones skidding treacherously under his feet.

How would he be received at the village, he wondered? He and Rolf undoubtedly shared similar features, but that in itself could prove a drawback and spark the need for an explanation; and how was he going to convince them that his intentions were good?

Shaun knew from his studies just how superstitious the old Saxons could be; heaven knows what they might make of a boy turning up who was so like one of their own, but with strange mannerisms and an even stranger accent!

But he knew his task was more complex and more difficult than that of simply being accepted and believed by the villagers. The biggest problem was going to be convincing them to pick up their weapons and follow him back to the bay, where they would have to fight yet another battle, and release prisoners they didn't even know existed.

Were they likely to do this on just his say-so?

Perhaps if he found Dirk...?

His wonderings undermined his concentration.

Negotiating a narrow track at the top of a slope, his foot slipped on loose rock and the next second he was plummeting, head over heels, down the incline. The motion of the fall in itself was enough to make him dizzy – he was tumbling and turning like a rag doll in a washing machine – but the fact that he cracked his head twice on the way down nearly finished him off.

He arrived groggily at the bottom, stars blazing before his eyes, and dragged himself into a sitting position against a boulder, his world spinning like a merry-go-round. A thin trickle of blood wandered down his cheek.

He remembered well the nausea and dizziness from his last tumble down a hill, but at least that time he had had grass to land on, not sharp, raking shale and hard rock. As before, very slowly, the spinning subsided, and he blinked away the fuzziness that blurred his vision. Bright spots danced before him, persisting even when his head had cleared completely, and it was several seconds before he realized that they had nothing to do with the effects of his fall. What he was seeing, he suddenly realized, was the far-off reflection of the late afternoon sun on metal.

The reflections were flittering up and down in a thin horizontal line. He judged it to be about a mile away; as he peered closer, the line shaped itself into the bobbing heads of a string of people – people carrying objects – and it was the objects they were carrying which were giving off the reflections.

Weapons!

Soldiers of some kind carrying weapons, swords, shields, some with helmets.

Vikings? They must be!

Had they sent men after him? No, that couldn't be the case, these men were coming from the opposite direction, and besides, they were a sizeable number, a hundred and fifty, maybe two hundred, he estimated, far too many to be chasing one escaping youth.

What then?

Were they a second Viking force marching to join those in the bay? But that didn't ring true, either; there was something about the unregimented, almost haphazard way in which they moved which ruled out the word "march". There was a purposefulness about their advance, but these were not militarily trained soldiers.

Shaun noted the direction from which they had come – roughly the same direction in which he had been heading before his fall – and suddenly his hopes leapt.

Could it be possible?

Could these be Saxons? Even, possibly the same Saxons he was hurrying to alert?

Another five minutes' wait strengthened his suspicions as the men drew closer and he saw clearly the round shields, the broad-bladed swords, and the clothing, mostly of animal skin; above all, the predominance of blond hair, worn long, cascading to their shoulders.

However, it was the dark, burly youth at the head of the column who caught Shaun's attention.

Dirk! But which Dirk?

Was this the imposter, the Omnian?

Was he leading these men into a trap?

Was this part of some elaborate plan to gain possession of the Phial? Shaun could think of no other reason why he should be where he was, unless, of course. . .

Was it the *real* Dirk?

Was the real Dirk alive as Rolf had been assured, or would the Omnian have had to kill Dirk to take over as him?

One thing was sure – Shaun was going to have to reveal himself, if only to be certain of this Dirk's intentions. Cautiously he stood, and began to walk towards the advancing column of men.

He was seen almost at once, and he watched as his sighting was passed back down the line from man to man.

Dirk looked up, and stiffened as he saw him, his hand going at once to the hilt of his sword.

The gap between them slowly closed, and Shaun could sense the unease and wariness.

At two hundred metres, Dirk turned and spoke to a tall man just behind him. The man raised his own sword high, and at once the Saxons stopped, many sat or squatted to rest, and Dirk himself strode forward, his weapon now unsheathed, to the spot where Shaun had come to a halt.

Shaun recognized Dirk for who he was as soon as he spoke: "What have you done with Rolf?" he spat.

For certain, this was the Dirk he remembered, the Dirk who had almost split him in two with a single blow when they had first met; the Dirk who had all the fire and alertness that the Omnian had found impossible to impersonate.

"Where is he?" barked Dirk sharply, and the point of his sword rose.

"Dirk," said Shaun, as calmly as he could. "Dirk, you're going to have to trust me. . ."

"Trust *you*?" snapped Dirk. "All this began the day you came!"

"Things may *seem* that way. . ." said Shaun.

"I was a fool to give you trust in the first place, and so was Rolf," cut in Dirk. "Who did ambush me in the trees, one of your friends?"

"That was nothing to do with me, and Rolf will tell you that himself!" Shaun replied, and he felt the anger and frustration rising in himself, too. "*If* we can get to him in time!"

A pause. "Another trick?"

"He's a prisoner . . . in the Viking camp."

"You lie! Rolf would die before he was taken!"

"Don't you listen to *anything*? He's a prisoner, and he needs our help!"

Dirk's eyes narrowed. "And Oswold?"

"He's there as well, just as Rolf thought he would be; and others, I don't know how many others. But they're about to break out of the compound they're held in, and they'll all be slaughtered – they're weaponless!"

Dirk hesitated. "How do I know this is the truth?"

"What do I have to gain?"

"The Phial that Rolf carries. If they are prisoners as you say, we could be your way of getting it."

"Dirk, you bonehead! Whilst we're arguing, Rolf's in danger!"

Still Dirk stood his ground.

"If it's the Phial I'm after, I could have taken it when Rolf offered it to me; you were there, you must remember."

Dirk licked his lips, uncertain.

"If you think there's nothing in what I say, why are you leading the village men there?"

"The men came of their own free will. Like Rolf, they want Oswold back . . . if indeed he is a prisoner."

"He is! Believe me! And now so is Rolf! I was on my way to find help! Well, now I've found help, are we going to stand here arguing, or are we going to help them?"

Shaun lowered his tone. "If you remember what we talked about, the three of us, about where I have come from, what Rolf is to me, then you'll realize that Rolf's safety, for me, is important. If it's important to you, you'll get there as fast as you can. Good grief, Dirk! You were on your way there, anyhow! Just hurry, will you!"

Dirk hesitated a second longer, then turned suddenly and trotted back to the head of the column where the tall man was waiting, watching proceedings.

Dirk spoke briefly to him, and the next minute, with a wave of his sword, he had brought the army to its feet. Another sword wave, and the whole band resumed its trek.

Dirk ran ahead to Shaun, and begrudgingly fell into step with him, as together they headed the troop unerringly in the direction of the Viking bay.

Retribution

Stones whistled along keen blades of axe and sword, as the Saxon village warriors honed their weapons to a fine cutting edge.

The whole band, 176 of them, lay just below the rim of the hill which led down to the bay which held the Viking encampment.

Cautiously, Shaun, Dirk, and Boton, the leader of the men in Oswold's absence, peered over the edge.

"See," said Shaun, "there's the compound." He pointed. "Those are the soldiers' tents; that is the Commander's tent, and over there is where they store the main bulk of their weapons between raids."

"Good," said Boton, and cast a look at the sun, now descending towards the sea. "We have an hour until twilight, they will be at their least alert then."

"But Oswold, and the other prisoners," put in Shaun, "they don't know we're here. They may break out before you decide to attack."

"Oswold also would choose the twilight, even more so if his men have no weapons. Fear not, he may not know we're here, but he is no fool."

Boton strode off to prepare his men, leaving Dirk and Shaun to consider the situation.

Dirk ate dried meat from his pouch, and offered some to Shaun.

"What do they think of me?" asked Shaun, accepting.

"The men?"

Shaun nodded. "They must wonder."

"They think you are of Rolf's family, from some far-off village." Dirk smiled wryly.

"Is that what you told them?"

Dirk nodded. "I just did not mention *how* far off."

Dirk estimated that the enemy had the advantage in numbers, there being approximately 250 to 300 of them. Boton, wisely, discounted help from the prisoners within the stockade, knowing that as well as being unarmed, many would be already wounded and unable to fight. It became more and more clear that the Saxon's main advantage in the coming battle would be their element of surprise.

If they could catch the enemy totally unaware, Dirk explained, they might be able to gain the upper hand

and force them into a position from which they couldn't recover.

Shaun's knowledge of Viking battle tactics impressed Dirk, and his willingness to share what he knew helped to convince Dirk that he was, indeed, sincere in his efforts to free Rolf and Oswold.

Boton wondered aloud to Dirk how Shaun knew so much about the ways of the enemy, but Dirk managed to convince him that Shaun's interest stemmed from a number of close encounters that he had had with the Vikings in his own village; a statement which held more truth than Dirk suspected.

"Whatever happens," Shaun told Boton, "we mustn't allow them to group."

Boton was obviously puzzled by this piece of advice. He had fought them not two days ago on the beach by the village, and had not seen them group at all.

"That was because *they* were attacking *you,*" explained Shaun. "When they have to defend themselves, they'll gather behind their shields in a wedge formation they call a 'Svinfylking', and we'll find it difficult to get at them."

As the minutes slipped by, and the time when the small Saxon army would rise and sweep over the ridge drew closer, Shaun's nervousness began to show almost as much as his apprehension. He didn't know if he would be expected to charge with them –

after all, he *was* swordless – but he eventually decided within himself that if he had to, then he would.

That was when Dirk brought him a sword. "Stain this red with Danish blood," he said.

Shaun tentatively gripped the handle, unable to believe the weight of the thing. "Thanks," he said, and managed a weak smile.

The Saxons were coming to their feet now, lining up, shoulder to shoulder just below the rim of the hill. Dirk took his place about a third of the way along the line, and Shaun had no alternative but to step up beside him, aware that his own countenance in no way reflected the wild grin and spirit that Dirk was displaying.

To either side stretched an array of every conceivable type of metal-bladed weapon – axe, sword and spear – brandished by some of the fiercest-looking individuals that Shaun could wish to see, and suddenly, surprisingly, he felt one of them.

His heritage seemed to well up inside him, and he felt what he realized the men around him must be feeling – a great indignation that others from a different land and with a different culture should dare to try to take from them, by force, what was theirs by birth.

He felt a hand upon his shoulder, and looking round, he saw that Boton had stepped up behind him and Dirk.

"You will be part of the rearguard," he said.

"Rearguard?" said Dirk.

"Some may try to escape over this hill," explained Boton, and so saying, he dragged the two of them from the line, and stepped quickly into the gap they left. They suddenly found themselves part of another line of maybe fifteen, all similarly chosen as part of the rearguard; all of them no older than Dirk or Shaun; one or two even younger, disqualified by lack of years from full combat.

Dirk was silently furious, like the others, who were unable to protest for fear of undermining the authority of Boton.

"Rearguard!" he spat. "I have seventeen summers!"

"Just our luck!" said Shaun, with a shake of his head, scarcely able to conceal his own feelings, which consisted mainly of relief.

Boton was on one knee now, sword held high.

For a long moment he held his pose, until he knew that each eye was upon him, and an utter silence had fallen. Not a twitch, not a fidget came from any man, each one tensed to take on the moment as it came. Shaun heard birds singing in the trees, so still had it become.

With a suddenness that took Shaun's breath away, Boton's arm dropped, the sword pointing the way forward, and almost as though they were tied together, every last man in the line ran forward and dropped over the rim of the hill, as effectively as if the earth had opened up and swallowed them.

The rearguard exchanged envious glances, and ran to the edge to watch as the little army descended.

For the first two hundred metres, they ran in silence save for the sound of their feet upon gravel and the swish of the odd bush as they passed.

Then, from somewhere on the left, began what sounded to Shaun like a low moan as the tension of waiting was released, and those most tense gave their feelings a voice.

The sound spread rapidly along the line, increasing in intensity and tone, until, by the time they were half-way down the hillside, the whole band were wailing as one man, a blood-curdling sound which bit fear into Shaun's heart.

From every part of the encampment startled heads were appearing; shouts of alarm and fear drifted up to them over the noise that the charging Saxons were making. Men ran to grab whatever weapons they could find, stunned by the suddenness of the attack, dismayed by the swiftness with which the horde of wild men were bearing down upon them.

Desperately, those who could tried to form some sort of defence, but it was all too late as, like a mighty wave breaking on the shore, the Saxons hurled themselves full upon their enemy, slashing, hacking, thrusting and battering their way on to the beach.

Then, with a thud, a whole section of the stockade

wall toppled on to the sand, the binding ropes severed by the dagger which Rolf had slipped earlier to his father, and a group of sixty or so prisoners poured from the gap.

Shaun and Dirk scanned the emerging group eagerly, anxious for any sign that Rolf might be amongst them, but nowhere did they see the familiar figure, and the worry arose that his injuries might, after all, have been fatal.

From the outset, it was clear that the prisoners' destination was the weapons tent; suddenly it became a mad scramble between them and those of the enemy who had been caught weaponless. From their vantage point on the ridge, Dirk and Shaun's small group saw the realization spread, almost like a tangible thing, amongst Saxon and Viking alike, that whoever managed to plunder the weapons tent first would gain an important advantage for their side.

Dirk nudged Shaun and pointed to the figure leading the prisoners' run; a well-proportioned man with the pace of a charging buffalo, his copper-red hair and beard streaming behind him as he ran. Shaun didn't need Dirk to tell him that this was Oswold, his paternal ancestor.

It soon became clear that the Vikings would reach the tent first; already the first half dozen were approaching the tent flap. As Oswold saw this also, he, and around fifteen others, put in a desperate burst of speed across the deep, strength-sapping sand.

"What are they doing?" cried Dirk in sudden dismay.

Oswold and his small band had veered to the right, and were fast approaching the *back* of the weapons tent. By this time, Vikings were pouring into it by the front flap. Reaching the tent, Oswold waited vital seconds until the last of his men were with him, then, with one dagger slash, he swiftly rent the cloth from top to bottom. Shaun could only imagine the surprise of the Vikings inside as Oswold and his men attacked from that unexpected quarter, bulldozing through the gap, followed by the rest of the prisoners as they arrived. The great tent heaved and billowed like a stricken animal as those inside fought hand to hand within the restricted space.

Elsewhere on the beach the fighting was truly ferocious. The more disciplined Danes and Norwegians, superior in number, tried again and again to group into defensive formations behind precious few shields, only to have these groups broken apart by the fury of the attacking Saxons.

Gradually, they retreated across the beach towards the sea.

From time to time, clusters of six or seven Vikings would make desperate charges into the ranks of the advancing Saxons, but such acts, brave though they were, were not enough to slow the forward thrust of their enemy.

The Saxons were stretched now, in a ragged double

line, the whole length of the beach, and hacking their way towards the sea. From the back of the Viking ranks, groups were beginning to break off and run to the boats, a sight which brought a cheer from the watching rearguard, and a roar of approval too, as Shaun explained how the boats had been damaged.

And yet, for every Viking that fled to the boats, there were three who stayed, and these, the most determined, now began to prove the most difficult to overcome. For the first time the Saxons found the impetus of their advance halted by ferocious opposition, and some of the most bitter fighting began to take place mid-beach. Dirk watched this most crucial part of the battle anxiously, growing more and more restless, his huge fist clasping and unclasping the handle of his sword as he fought to control his impatience. His fight was almost as hard as the Saxons' on the beach. Eventually, it was plain he could contain himself no longer, and he turned to the others, a fiendish look in his eyes.

"I see none escaping over this hill we are guarding," he said.

The others were quick to agree – all the escaping was being done by boat.

"A pity to waste fifteen good men up here," he continued. "What say you?"

Again, a chorus of agreement, and Shaun's heart raced with the prospect of what he could see was about to happen. Could it be possible that, after years of study, countless hours of reading about battles such as this, he was about to actually charge into one, a *real* one, and fight to the death alongside his own ancestors?

"Why do we hesitate?" yelled Dirk, and with that, he led the charge down the slope, closely followed by the others, and Shaun, his own spirits soaring on the tide of battle, the blood pounding in his temples, went with them.

The battle within the weapons' tent had been resolved, and even as Shaun ran, Oswold and his men emerged from the front flap, in pursuit of the beaten Vikings, each Saxon armed to the teeth with Viking swords, spears and daggers. They chased the Vikings down as far as the water's edge, then turned, to come up behind those who were still putting up such fierce resistance, trapping them just up from the shallows.

The boats were filling fast as more and more of the enemy realized the futility of carrying on a fight that was already lost. The first longboat began to pull away, and two more were about to do so, as Dirk's small band threw themselves into the ranks, their young arms flailing in support of their elders.

Shaun found himself torn between a desire to do well, to help, and an unwillingness to kill or injure anyone. At the back of his mind all the while was the thought that his presence here in the battle was yet another intrusion in time, he wasn't meant to be here, and certainly, no one should die because of him. That could change any number of things. Instinctively, Shaun found himself flitting from combat to combat, assisting any Saxon who seemed to need assistance, using his sword in a defensive, as opposed to an aggressive, way, parrying a blow here, knocking away an enemy sword there, dodging the whistling strokes aimed at his own head, being careful not to interfere in a way which would determine the outcome of any particular fight, and all the while asking himself if all this was really happening.

In this manner, he made his way along the ranks towards that side of the beach which contained the compound. He could see Dirk in the thick of it. For Dirk, and the rest of the Saxons, this was a fight for survival – kill or be killed.

Shaun threw a glance towards the compound, and what he saw made his heart leap. Dirk was close by; Shaun grabbed his arm and pointed to the gap in the stockade wall.

A number of those prisoners who had been unable to join the battle had arranged themselves against the outer wall of the stockade to watch the spectacle, and there, amongst them, leaning wearily against a post, was Rolf. His chest and left arm were roughly bandaged with sacking, and he was obviously in pain, for he broke suddenly into coughing and he held his ribs before turning and limping back into the compound and out of their sight.

A movement amongst the boulders to the left of the stockade caught Shaun's eye; a figure was moving stealthily in the direction of the compound, and at first they thought it was a lone Viking warrior. If indeed it was, how the man had managed to get behind Saxon lines was not immediately clear, but it was apparent that his destination, for some reason, was the compound itself. What was just as apparent was that he had his eyes fixed firmly on the back of the retreating Rolf, intent, it would seem, on approaching him unseen.

The remaining injured prisoners were moving down towards the fighting now, encouraging their men to even greater efforts, none of them aware of the menacing figure behind them, nor of the threat he seemed to pose to Rolf.

Dirk sprang into action, followed closely by Shaun, and together they ploughed through the treacle sand towards the compound. There was no mistaking the man's intentions, but why Rolf? Of all the prisoners in evidence, why was he stalking him in particular?

Suddenly Dirk slid to a halt, and Shaun skidded into the back of him.

"Dirk! What do you think you're..." began Shaun, but his voice trailed off as he saw the stunned expression on Dirk's face.

Shaun followed his gaze.

No wonder Dirk was staring so unbelievably; this was no Viking.

Dirk was watching himself!

Shaun drew breath sharply as he saw the Omnian lookalike slip furtively through the gap in the stockade wall.

Parting

"Dirk!" Shaun had to shout to get through Dirk's bewilderment.

Dirk had been totally unprepared to confront the image of himself; the sword had dropped from his hand, and the shock was so great that it took Shaun a full minute to shake him back to reality. Even when the fear and incredulity had finally left his eyes, he was still at a loss as to how he might even *ask* about what he had seen.

Shaun's new anxiety for Rolf's safety forbade him time to explain and, much as he hated to prolong Dirk's confusion, he knew that the priority now was to get to Rolf as quickly as possible.

"Dirk . . . I'll explain! I promise! Right now we *have* to get to Rolf!"

Dirk shook his head, blinked away the stupor, and watched as Shaun raced towards the compound, calling over his shoulder as he went, "Quickly!"

With an effort, Dirk gathered his wits and his sword, and ran after him.

Certainly the lookalike would be after the Phial, thought Shaun, and to lose that, after all he had been through, would be a disaster that he would find hard to come to terms with.

It was, for one thing, the only passage home that he knew of.

Oblivious to the noise of the battle being fought to its conclusion by the water's edge, they ran as though in a dream, the clinging sand giving them legs of lead, until breathlessly, they rounded the stockade posts and in through the gap.

They were not expecting to see what it was they saw. Rolf was sitting on a low rock, and sitting on another, facing him, as calmly as you please, was Kal the Omnian, looking almost more like Dirk than Dirk himself.

They were talking as though they had all the time in the world.

Rolf's face lit with pleasure and relief as Dirk and Shaun appeared, and he staggered painfully to his feet as they approached.

Kal also rose, but stepped back apprehensively.

Dirk's eyes never left Kal's face, even when Rolf embraced him, and as Shaun helped Rolf back to the rock he had been sitting on, the two identical boys faced each other, one scowling menacingly, the other showing no emotion at all.

They were true mirror-images, down to the last detail, and Shaun could sense the resentment building up inside the hot-tempered Dirk as he eyed the impostor. When he finally spoke, Dirk's voice carried menace. "Time, is it not, Shaun," he said, his gaze full on Kal, "for the explanation you promised."

Shaun rattled his brain for some sort of starting point. How could he possibly explain the full story to either Dirk *or* Rolf? Rolf seemed to have come to some sort of understanding with the Omnian; how much of it all did Rolf know already?

It was Rolf, as it happened, who broke the silence.

"His name is Kal," he said, "and he will do us no harm."

Dirk swung his gaze to Rolf, considered a while, then nodded briefly in acceptance of Rolf's statement, though his hand remained crooked around the hilt of his sword.

"He is from your time?" Dirk asked of Shaun.

Shaun took a breath, sighed. "My time, yes," he said, then shrugged, "but not my world."

Now it was Rolf's turn to shrug in answer to Dirk's questioning look.

Kal took a pace forward.

"I think I may be the one to tell the story," he said.

"By the gods, he even talks with my voice!" muttered Dirk.

Kal's story was a revealing one indeed and, to his credit, Shaun noted that he couched it in terms readily understandable to Rolf and Dirk, with regard for the simplicity of the lifestyle they were used to.

Kal had been orphaned during one of Omnia's many wars, and kept (rather than cared for) by the military who had brought him up to be an agent, a spy, an assassin whose job it was to further the ambitions of the cruel rulers of Omnia.

"To retrieve the Phial was my first mission," he said, "and I failed. Failure is not tolerated by my leaders."

"Do you not mean," said Rolf, "that you *chose* to fail?"

Kal lowered his eyes and shuffled uncomfortably.

"How could that be?" put in Dirk. "No one chooses to fail at anything they do."

"When Shaun disappeared," went on Rolf, "when you and I were alone in the water, no, even before that, you had the chance to kill us both and take the Phial. Why did you not?"

Kal hesitated before answering. "Why did I not kill Dirk when I duplicated his body? I know not. Something told me it was the wrong thing to do."

"And yet, you were trained to kill," said Shaun.

"With you three, it was different," said Kal. "I watched you, even before I took on the look of Dirk, even as you arrived in this time," he said to Shaun. "I saw how Rolf saved you from Dirk's sword, and I wondered why. I was curious. Then later, I saw that you all had something which I had not seen before, something which I now know is called friendship. All I knew was how to kill, how to bring life to an end. You had something that made life meaningful, better. When I saw how you looked at each other, heard how you spoke to each other, saw how you cared for each other, I knew that friendship was a thing I had to learn, a thing too precious to be killed."

Dirk gave a short laugh, but when he spoke there was sympathy, rather than irony in his voice. "You come to kill, you are surrounded by people who *are* killing, yet you decide that to kill is wrong."

"To kill without reason *is* wrong," said Kal. "I know that now, and I learned that only by being with you. You kill only because you have to, to defend yourselves and your friends, your families."

Dirk nodded agreement.

Kal continued. "And you fight with something called honour, with 'bravery', against the bad of your world. In my world we know nothing like that. We live to kill. You kill to live. That is the difference."

The sounds of battle out on the beach had died now, replaced by yells and shouts of victory, cries of triumph. The rejoicings would last a little while longer, but soon now, they knew, Oswold would be returning for his son.

Shaun recognized the moment as the one he had been working towards since his arrival; if ever there was going to be a right time for him to leave, it had to be now.

Rolf, too, had been reading the signs, and the unspoken agreement that the time had come was clear to see on his face. Sadly he took from his pouch the gleaming Phial, balancing it across his palm.

"And you, Kal?" he said.

Kal shrugged. "I cannot go back, my leaders would kill me as a failure; and I have no wish to end my life just at the moment when I have discovered how it should be lived."

"But you cannot stay, looking . . . looking like me," said Dirk. "Who would understand?"

Kal looked suitably sorry. "An Omnian can change his body but once within his lifetime. Now I am Dirk, I must remain Dirk."

The others exchanged bewildered glances.

"Then we have a problem," said Rolf, pointing with his chin to the gap in the stockade wall. Oswold and a band of men were marching towards the stockade across the beach.

In less than a minute they would arrive.

It was obvious to Shaun, if not to the others, what he would have to do. "Kal," he said, "quickly – stand by me."

Hope rose in Kal's eyes as the essence of Shaun's intentions became clear.

"Neither of us belongs in this time," said Shaun.

"Will the power be strong enough for two?" asked Kal.

"We're about to find out." And Shaun wrapped an arm around Kal's neck.

He looked across to Rolf, at the face so like his own, at the boy whom he seemed to have known for a lifetime; the boy he should really never have met, and who he would never, ever see again.

As in death, this was a parting that was final, and he felt the tears prickle the back of his eyes.

Rolf stood, and stepped up to him, and they embraced warmly. "Goodbye, Shaun," he said. "You will not be easily forgotten."

"Dirk, look after him," called Shaun, and as Dirk nodded, he reached, anxious now for the goodbyes to be over, and snatched the Phial from Rolf's hand, offering one end of it to Kal.

"Kal," called Dirk, "good luck. Take care of my body!"

Shaun felt a tingling sensation and a tugging from somewhere above his head as though a giant magnet were attracting him, and then, slowly, Rolf, Dirk and the world around him faded.

19

Back

"Boost power!" Jarrod again impatiently knocked aside the hand that was too slow to respond, and operated the Impulsator himself.

"Two coming through!" announced Tulkan on the monitor control.

"What?" The surprise rang clearly in Jarrod's voice as he strode to the console, peering over the man's shoulder.

"Phasedionic Compensator! Enhance the sensitivity mode!" Tulkan wrestled to input his own instructions.

Jarrod opened a communications channel at the touch of a sensorpad. "Security!" he said, grimly. "Report to transfer pod immediately!"

He had no means of knowing who, or what, had

been transported with Shaun, no way of knowing if the person – or animal – had accidentally been in contact with him when the transfer took place, or even if he had been forced, against his will, to bring him or her. If it had been a decision by Shaun, it was a risky one, and all Jarrod's attention now was taken with the task of generating the extra power that was needed to get them both back safely through time.

Once that had been taken care of, *then* he could begin to worry about the identity of the extra traveller. Deftly, he and Tulkan fought with the controls, feeding impulses from Shaun's transfer energies to the chromosome mass of his companion, counteracting the drag on their forward speed with short bursts of alignment energy, by superimposing Shaun's image over the fast-fading image of Rolf, reversing the physiological thrust that had been used earlier to draw the two people together.

For long seconds, it was touch and go, and for one moment he thought they were going to fall short of their year, and then the danger was past, the orange light which indicated "critical" winked out, and Jarrod sighed a breath he hadn't realized he'd been holding as he saw that Shaun, and whoever was with him, was coasting to safety.

Swiftly, he ran the distance to the transfer pod, and positioned himself by the viewing monitor as the spectrum of lights began their countdown sequence. As the pure white blurred and began to fade, Jarrod saw that it was another human who had accompanied Shaun, a boy of his own age – but who? And why?

He noted that Shaun didn't seem in any way threatened by his companion, but nevertheless, care had to be taken, and until such time as he could see the newcomer face to face and read his thoughts, Jarrod could only guess at his motives.

He motioned for two security men to position themselves by the hatch. Sensors showed that both travellers were in need of some medical attention; there was early evidence of plasma shock, and a tissue scan at the molecular level showed a possibility of some microcrystaline damage due to the added strain of dual transport.

The whole pod would need to be de-bacterialized and tested for harmful inclusions before they could exit. Meanwhile, the Phial had to be recovered and sent on its way without the loss of any more time.

Jarrod opened a communication. "Shaun," he said, "are you all right?"

"Am I back?" asked Shaun.

"You're back," said Jarrod.

"I've got someone with me..."

Jarrod cut in before he could say any more. "Explanations later, Shaun," he said. "The Phial..."

"It's here," said Shaun, and held it up.

"You'll see a handle in the wall near you – pull it."

Shaun did so, and a hinged compartment fell open.

"Put the Phial in the compartment, and close it up."

Again Shaun did as instructed, and heard a hiss as the Phial was ejected into a tray on Jarrod's side of the pod.

Almost before it had stopped rolling, it was scooped up by a waiting crew member who ran with it to the main control room.

Jarrod allowed himself a smile before turning his attention to the youth to whom he would be eternally grateful – and to the problem he seemed to have brought with him.

Shaun had been relieved and delighted to learn that he had only been away for ten minutes of real time, and whilst the sterilization of the pod and the biological repair to its occupants was taking place, Jarrod went ahead to a reception room, comfortably furnished, and amply supplied with refreshments, to await their arrival.

He had a nagging apprehension about the youth that Shaun had brought with him. He had noticed a look in the boy's eyes that had told him a number of things; it told him, for a start, that he was not a native of the Year of the Phial – he sat too comfortably for that, appeared too used to the position he found himself in. An Anglo-Saxon from that time would be far more frightened and confused than this boy was.

Furthermore, tests taken by Tulkan had shown Tetrion traces in the young man's bloodstream.

Tetrion was a compound found only in beings from Jarrod's solar system. By the time Tulkan joined him in the reception room, Jarrod already knew what he had come to tell him.

Shaun had returned with the Omnian!

They had no time for further discussion before Shaun and Kal entered the room.

They were clean, refreshed and alert; Shaun's translation device had been removed painlessly from his ear, and he was in clothes similar to those he had worn at the start of his journey, whilst Kal had been given a zip-suit to wear.

Kal's wary expression mirrored the apprehension he felt, as he stepped forward of his own accord. "My name is Kal," he said, evenly. "And I am..."

"An Omnian." Tulkan finished off the sentence for him, his tone patronizing. "We know. You are the agent who was sent to recover the Phial."

Kal nodded. "What will you do with me?" he asked.

"What would you have me do, Kal?" asked Jarrod.

"He belongs on Omnia," snapped Tulkan. "We should let Omnia have him back; we all know what they think of failures."

"We wouldn't have the Phial without him!" cut in Shaun, his anger rising.

"Oh? A traitor, too?" mocked Tulkan.

Jarrod turned sharply to rebuke Tulkan, but before he could speak, Kal spoke for himself.

"No. Not a traitor. Someone who has no longer any loyalties to Omnia. I did what I did only because I now know different."

"Kal," Jarrod said gently, "it occurs to me that since you now have a human body, you have little choice but to try to make the best of it. What do you say to that?"

"I have a human body," said Kal, "but more than that, I believe that I am developing a human spirit."

Tulkan scoffed, but Jarrod ignored him, impressed by Kal's directness. His instincts told him that Kal's words were a true product of his mind's output; that he wasn't putting on a performance to save his life.

What he said, Jarrod was sure he meant.

"What makes you think that you can achieve this human spirit?" he asked.

"I don't know that I can," replied Kal. "I only know that I want to more than anything else."

"Why should we believe you?" Tulkan came back. "Omnians are known liars the universe over."

Kal bridled. "You'd obviously prefer me dead," he said. "It may interest you to know that I would prefer to be dead if it meant that I could no longer strive to be a human in spirit as well as body. If you think that I want to remain here only to save my life, then, please, transport me to Omnia now." He turned to face Jarrod. "All I ask is that you transfer me to a time, any time, here on Earth. Somewhere I can continue to learn."

Jarrod was warming to the boy. His attitude was admirable, but still he probed him, searching for incongruities, anything that might hint at deceit.

"There are other worlds, Kal, where your body would be accepted, some even in your own galaxy. Worlds more pleasant, less complicated. Why Earth?"

"Earth alone has humans of the kind I want to be," replied Kal. "That is the only answer I can give."

Jarrod's expression softened. "Would Shaun have anything to do with that decision?" he asked.

"Everything," said Kal, "and all humans, friend or enemy, that I have met on my mission. I have learned through them to care for others, but there is more to learn, things I have no names for..."

"We will talk more," smiled Jarrod. "Now, if you would both leave us..."

As the door slid across behind them, Jarrod turned to Tulkan.

"Once an Omnian, always an Omnian," began Tulkan. "They may be able to change their bodies, but..."

Jarrod held up a hand to silence him. "Tulkan," he said, flatly. "I have never liked you, you have never liked me. And, until now, there has been nothing either of us could do about that."

"What do you mean, 'until now'?"

"The retrieval of the Phial is not the only good news to have come about today, and the heavens alone know how short of good news we have been this past two moonruns."

"Come to the point, Jarrod, what good news?"

"Concerning the governorship of the planet now that the Governor has sadly died."

Tulkan blinked rapidly, suspicion creeping into his tone. "You have an advantage over me, Jarrod. I have heard nothing of a new appointment."

Jarrod savoured the moment – he knew he shouldn't, but it felt good. He tried hard to contain the pleasure it gave him to reveal to Tulkan what he knew. "Word came that the Council of Grava have agreed to a joint governorship of the planet."

Tulkan licked his lips nervously. "A ... a *joint* governorship? How ... how interesting."

"By Commander Drago and myself," continued Jarrod.

Tulkan's jaw visibly dropped. "I ... I had no idea..." he stammered.

"The new Grava will have no room for those whose hearts are closed to change, and I think, Tulkan, that your heart is a very closed place indeed."

"But ... but it's thanks to my methods that the Phial..."

Again Jarrod dismissed his words. "Your efforts will receive the acknowledgement they deserve, I can assure you," he said, "but the point of what I'm saying is that your services for our government will no longer be required – ever."

And Home

Shaun, with Jarrod and Kal, was standing at the entrance to a large, brightly-lit tunnel, his watch back on his wrist reading ten minutes later than the last time he had worn it. The second hand wasn't moving, but that, he knew, didn't account for much under the circumstances.

The tunnel stretched before him, like every tunnel he'd ever seen, except that he had been told that home was at the end of this one and, after all that had happened, who was he to argue with that?

He had said his goodbyes, and all that there was left to do was turn and walk into the tunnel – except that he was finding it wasn't as easy as all that. His journey had been filled with danger, and there had been times when he had been convinced that he wouldn't survive it, but for all that, it had been a great adventure, and one which a part of him didn't want to end.

The events of the past few hours? days? minutes? kaleidoscoped in his mind, the hundred things he'd done, (or had he?) seemed now more like a dream than any kind of reality, and the only evidence he had that anything at all had taken place was that, for the moment, two of the people he had shared it all with were standing next to him.

The leaving of Rolf and Dirk had been sad, but mercifully quick. This departure was different in that he had had time to think, to dwell on what it meant, and he knew it was so final. Once he'd severed himself from Jarrod he knew the adventure was at an end, that all the people he'd been privileged to be with would be there no longer, and, anxious as he was to resume normality, to savour the luxury of being safe and in familiar surroundings, he felt a sadness.

And how would he feel about things once he'd taken the plunge and left them behind?

How dream-like would it all appear then? Once back in his own world, would he even remember what had gone on considering that it had all happened within ten minutes of time as he knew it? Would all his memories condense into that time span, and if so, would they all become just fleeting micro-thoughts with no space in which to establish themselves?

Jarrod sensed his uncertainty.

"Nothing you can do will prolong the moment, Shaun," he said. "There is a future waiting for you."

"It's just that..." Shaun began.

"You want to take the memory of what you've been through with you?"

"Yes ... yes, I do. But how much can be crammed into ten miserable minutes?"

"Do you remember all of it now?" asked Jarrod.

"Oh, yes, every detail. But once the time-stretch finishes..."

"The time-stretch finished two minutes ago, when we came out here. What you remember now is exactly what you'll remember all your life."

Shaun smiled. He felt relieved. Now he was ready to go home.

"Enjoy the rest of your life, Shaun," said Jarrod.

"I'll try," replied Shaun, and hesitated, a thumb in his belt. "I don't suppose we'll ever meet again."

"Ever is a long time," smiled Jarrod, and dug into the pocket of his suit. "Please, take this."

Shaun found himself accepting the object that Jarrod held out to him; a phial like the one he'd chased through history, but smaller, maybe half the size, and still with that same, silky smoothness he'd come to recognize.

"A souvenir?" Shaun asked. It seemed a little

inappropriate for Jarrod's style to be giving away mementos.

"Let's just say it'll keep us in touch," Jarrod said.

Shaun gave a puzzled frown, and pocketed it. A final handshake, then he strode into the tunnel.

The echoes from his shoes resounded from the walls, blak! blak! blak! It was almost like being inside a huge steel drum. He looked back once, and waved, and Jarrod and Kal watched him until he was just a speck in the distance.

"A remarkable young man," said Jarrod, and turned away, an arm around Kal's shoulder. He was thinking of a little boy years ago who had run into the Cephos woods and called his name. A boy who could have been as tall and as praiseworthy as either the one who had just left, or the one who now walked with him.

"Tell me, Kal," he said, "in time, when you have studied, and learned, from humans, would you be interested in assisting me on Grava? I have a home you could live in."

Shaun became aware of a distant roar in competition with the hollow ring of his shoes on the tunnel floor, and the further he strode down the bright passage, the louder that roar became.

He quickened his pace, anxious now to reach the tunnel's end, and as the roaring increased, so the resonance of his footsteps decreased.

Then suddenly, his footsteps were no longer echoing at all. He felt a breeze on his face; the tunnel wall had disappeared and had become a simple brick arch over his head, springing up, stem-like, from the roadway at his feet.

With a shock of recognition, he realized that the arch was part of the railway viaduct at the end of his street; the roaring that of a train passing directly above him.

He was home.

The phial in his pocket rubbed against his leg, and he took it out, suddenly anxious to be sure that it was still there, that it, as well as he, had survived the journey back. What had Jarrod meant about it keeping them in touch? Did he mean in a symbolic sense? Somehow, he didn't think so.

The train rattled into the distance, to be replaced by the hum and growl of modern day activity, distant car engines, an aeroplane droning in the sky, a dog's bark. A hundred different sounds assailed his ears, sounds he realized he hadn't actually taken notice of before; the sound of civilization, more obtrusive than he remembered it, and so different from the quiet, clean world of Rolf and Dirk that he'd been a part of for . . . he looked at his watch, and saw that the second hand was sweeping around . . . thirteen minutes? Twelve?

"Shaun, is that you, love?" His mother's voice rang through from the kitchen as he entered the front door.

She came through, wiping her hands, and set about laying the table.

"I was just getting worried about you."